NOT ANOTHER DUKE

THE KENT'S ROW DUCHESSES

BOOK TWO

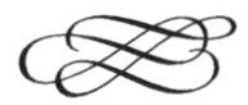

JESS MICHAELS

For Michael, always and forever.

CHAPTER 1

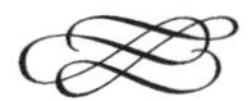

Fall 1815

Roarke Desmond made a slow count of ten in his head and schooled his expression so that his utter disgust with his surroundings would not be clear. It was something he had been doing for most of his life when he was forced to visit his three hateful cousins, so he was very good at it. After all, he had no other choice.

"Do you remember little Gregory Parson?" his cousin Thomas was asking now, drawing Roarke back into the conversation.

Roarke inclined his head. "Er, yes. I think so. He lived out near your father's estate in Sidmouth, did he not?"

"*My* estate in Sidmouth," Thomas snapped, and Roarke clenched his jaw.

His eldest cousin had been impossible to take for his entire life. Thomas was always lording his elevated position over Roarke and anyone else he deemed less than worthy. Roarke had hoped he might grow out of such immature nastiness, but Thomas's entitled posturing had only increased in the three years since Roarke's uncle Stuart had died and his oldest cousin had become duke.

There was almost no bearing him now.

"Of course," Roarke soothed with a stifled sigh. "Your estate. What about him?"

"Do you know that Gertrude saw him scuttling about *Cheapside* the other day?" Thomas pivoted his head and speared his younger sister with a glare. "Tell him."

Gertrude had been staring into her tea, apparently as bored by all this as Roarke was, but now she lifted her gaze and gave a smile. It seemed cruelty was a trait all his cousins shared. "I did. He owns a shop there—can you imagine?"

Roarke drew in a long breath and once again schooled his tone. "It's a very successful mercery, if I recall. They import and sell the finest fabrics for furnishings. He and his wife run the shop."

All three of his cousins pulled a face, clearly unimpressed by the success of their old neighbor's business. But of course, so many of their rank were like that.

"Well, that's quite a fall from his upbringing," his third cousin, Philip, snorted as he chewed a biscuit from the tea set on the sideboard, little flecks of food flying from his mouth as he did so. "Then again, I suppose you know about that, don't you, cousin?"

The three of them laughed, as if this were good-natured ribbing, not cruel taunting. Roarke shifted in his seat. It wasn't as if he could deny the charge. He had certainly fallen far further than the man they were discussing. Although his connection to their family was on their mother's side, rather than their duke father, Roarke had still been raised with a level of privilege and expectation.

Both of which had been ruined over the last two years. His father had started it. Francis Desmond had been a kind man, a good man, but he was a dreamer. Sometimes that led him to be too trusting or too certain of an investment. He had whittled down every bit of money he had available to him by the time of his death in a carriage accident.

Roarke had done little better. His mother had been left behind and was not well. She needed constant care—some days she didn't even know who he was. Desperate, he'd followed in his father's footsteps, trying to catch up, trying to make enough that he could take care of his responsibilities. To keep her comfortable.

He had failed. Almost as spectacularly as his father had. Which was why he had to come here and listen to his snobby cousins gossip about people they knew and be generally unpleasant. He was, for all intents and purposes, a dependent person now. If he wanted their continued financial support, this was the only way.

His stomach turned at the thought and he set his own teacup down. "What are your plans now that the Season is coming to an end?" he asked, hoping this would change the subject from one vapid subject to another more palatable one.

"I would say I was happy to be returning to the country estate," Thomas groaned, and rolled his eyes at his siblings. "But I feel as though we are always working there to undo the damage that dreadful woman did before our dear father's death."

Roarke wrinkled his brow. "Are you talking about the dowager? Your stepmother?"

Gertrude slammed her cup down on the sideboard and let out a little pained cry. "My God, but I hate that she gets to claim any title that has to do with my father. Hateful, wretched thing. She married my father at his lowest point and did everything she could to turn him against us."

"She used her grubby hands and smutty charms to grab everything she could," Philip agreed, and Roarke recoiled. He was shocked his cousin would use such plain language with Gertrude in the room. She was a lady, after all, and an unmarried one at that. It was unseemly.

He shook his head. "I know she was a good deal younger than your father—"

"Younger than me," Gertrude said. "By two years. So what does that tell you?"

Roarke didn't respond. He had some thoughts about what that said, most of which were a bit more judgmental of his uncle than the young lady he had wed. After all, women had fewer choices when it came to their fate. And from what he knew of the lady, she had come from a good family, one that would see a union with a duke, old or young, as a triumph for her.

And though he hadn't spent much time with his uncle after the death of his aunt, his father's sister, the few times he'd bumped into him at a club or gathering, Uncle Stuart had seemed vastly content with his choice of second wife. He always spoke warmly of her, at least, in their brief encounters.

"But you know, you must have seen her," Thomas was continuing, and Roarke realized he had blocked out much of their complaints.

He forced himself back to the present. "Er, no. I never met the lady, I'm afraid. Though you've made it no secret how little you three think of her, before or since your father's death."

"I should think we wouldn't," Philip said, his brow lowering. "After all she has taken from us. Her settlement was outrageous. Absolutely outrageous. If I had been in charge—"

"Philip," Thomas said sharply, and Roarke's younger cousin snapped his mouth shut with a sullen glare.

Roarke couldn't help but look around the opulent home they all sat in at present. He didn't think his cousins were hurting for funds, no matter how much their uncle had gifted for the widow he left behind.

"It has been three years since his death," Roarke said as gently as he could. "And it seems the lady is no longer in your lives. Thomas is happily in place as duke, so he makes the decisions for the future of the family, and there were no children from the second union to take anything from you. I am surprised you are still so bitter toward his second wife."

Thomas let out a long sigh and the three cousins exchanged a look heavy with meaning. It immediately put Roarke on edge. He knew that look, had seen it dozens of times as a child. It almost always meant his cousins had a plan of some kind, usually a cruel one, and they wished for him to be part of it. Probably so he could be blamed if the entire thing went wrong.

And once again Roarke cursed the fact that he had to grovel to them for money three times a year for the upkeep of his ill mother. Why had he not been more prudent? Why had he inherited his own late father's penchant for risk when it came to bright ideas of the future? There had been so little left to inherit, but perhaps if he had been prudent and guarded, he might be in a different position now.

"Well, I suppose we are thinking of the cruel grasping of his wretched wife all the more lately because of the terms of settlement we just discovered only this week," Thomas said.

"Only this week," Roarke said flatly. "You are telling me that you are still finding new terms of inheritance after all this time?"

"Yes," Thomas said, his tone getting a bit sharper. "You have no idea what we have endured. How hard it is to go through papers and papers, trying to sort out the whims of a father."

Roarke bit his tongue. They never had considered his father much of anything, despite his being their mother's brother, so of course they wouldn't see his death and the ripples that had come from it as the same thing.

"Hmmm" was all Roarke responded.

"Dearest Papa was far too kind," Gertrude continued, moving closer to Roarke. He realized they were all doing it, almost surrounding him, and his stomach turned. "There was an additional term in regard to our stepmother, and it will come into effect very soon if we do not stop it."

"And what is the term?" Roarke asked, trying to back away from the circling vultures, but only serving to edge himself farther into the corner of the room.

"Flora will inherit an additional ten thousand pounds if she reaches the third year of her widowhood without remarrying or taking a lover," Thomas said, his mouth twisting with disgust.

Roarke's head spun a moment. Ten thousand pounds. Great

God, he came to beg for one percent of that amount just to stay afloat, just to keep his mother fed and minded.

"It's not much of a sum," Philip sneered. "But that bitch hasn't earned it."

Yet again Roarke flinched at the crude language his cousin used to address his stepmother and in front of his maiden sister. "Your father seems to have felt differently," he said softly. "He must have cared for her a great deal in order to wish to protect her so thoroughly, as I imagine she must have inherited a tidy sum at this death."

"Fifteen thousand," Gertrude sneered. "Half again over what *I* inherited."

Roarke shook his head. Great God, but these people were so entirely separated from reality. They lived like kings and compared themselves to paupers. They hated a woman for taking from them, when it seemed there were unlimited resources available left to them by a caring father who had stewarded his unentailed finances carefully to protect his family. *All* his family.

Roarke despised them for it.

He smoothed his coat and then forced a sympathetic smile. "I am sorry to hear of your woes, cousins. I imagine you must feel great frustration over this news. I feel as though I am intruding now on your grief. Perhaps I should go and we can meet again another—"

"No," Thomas interrupted, arching a brow and glowering at Roarke in what he could only assume was his cousin's attempt at a *lord of the manor* expression. "You came here to ask for our assistance, as you do several times a year."

"The money is for my mother," Roarke began, but his cousin lifted his hand.

"I don't give a damn about your mother," he snapped. "*She* was not related to us through blood." Roarke clenched his fists at his sides but managed not to react in any other way as his cousin continued, "You receive a sum from the family at *our* pleasure. *Our* discretion. I've never asked you for repayment, have I?"

"No." Roarke managed the one word through clenched teeth. "You are very kind."

"Do you feel you owe me?" Thomas pressed, his eyes lighting with further cruelty.

Roarke bent his head, his breath coming rough. "You are talking about repayment, I suppose. I don't know how you expect such a thing when you are so keenly aware of my circumstances. I thought lording it over me would be enough for you, as it has always been a pleasure to you to do so."

"Watch your tongue, cousin, or it might be watched for you," Philip said, edging closer. "The duke is talking to you."

Roarke forced himself to lift his gaze back to Thomas's and held there. "What do you want?"

"Nothing dire," Thomas said, his tone dripping with false reassurance. "Nothing financial, so it will not be a trial to you. I am only asking that you investigate our stepmother. She didn't know you, so she wouldn't suspect if you did a little snooping into her life."

"Investigate what?" Roarke sputtered.

"She *must* be whoring herself out," Gertrude spat.

Roarke jerked his attention toward her. Here he had been surprised at the blunt language of his male cousins in front of her, but she was just as vulgar when it came to her stepmother.

"She has to have a lover," Gertrude continued. "She probably had one while she was watching my father die in the bed beside her. And now she hides his...or even *their*...existence just so she can milk a little more away from Papa's estate where it belongs."

Roarke pushed past his cousins at last, his distaste finally overriding any duty he felt here. "No," he said, walking toward the door. "Absolutely not."

"Five hundred pounds."

Roarke stopped as Thomas said the sum. He stared at the door, his escape. He usually got three hundred pounds a year from this lot, barely enough to scrape by and cover his mother's carer. With an extra five hundred he could make her more comfortable, even give her a few niceties.

He swallowed and turned back to stare at the vultures who called themselves his family. They were smiling at him now. They already knew the trap was sprung, and he hated them and himself for the fact that it was true.

"You cared for your uncle, didn't you?" Thomas asked.

Roarke pursed his lips. "Yes," he choked out, and it was true. As a child he'd been close to his uncle, who had always been kind to him. But once his aunt had died, all that had changed. Thanks in part, he believed, to the very cousins who he stood before now. They had pushed him out and he had lost the bond to his uncle, except for fleeting conversations when they found each other at the same club.

"Flora was a monster," Thomas continued, his tone serious. "Whatever you think of us, know that to be true. She took advantage of him in his old age, she played him for a fool all for what she could gain from him after his death. If you do this, you would be defending his honor."

Roarke drew in a long breath. He had to give it to his cousins, they were experts at manipulation. Yes, the money was a tantalizing carrot to dangle in front of him, but the idea that he could do the right thing was even more attractive. If they were even a fraction correct that his late uncle's young wife was using the situation for her own gain, then perhaps she *did* deserve to have her schemes uncovered.

And if not...well, at least Roarke knew he wouldn't lie about it. Not like some other investigators his cousins might hire if he refused them. He could be a dispassionate judge of the circumstances and either deliver the dowager from the lies her stepchildren told, or condemn her for being a mercenary and using his uncle.

Either way, when he told himself this, convinced himself, it made him feel a little less guilty. "When do I get the money?"

"I will put half in your account today," Thomas said. "Along with the other amount we agreed to earlier in our meeting. And when you have given me your report, you'll have the other half."

Roarke folded his arms. "What if I find that the lady is innocent of the charge that she has taken a secret lover?"

All three of his cousins scrunched their faces as if in disbelief. "There is no way she isn't," Philip said. "Not with her beauty."

Roarke's stomach turned as Thomas flashed his brother a salacious grin. "What if it's not true?" he insisted.

Thomas threw up his hands. "Then you get the rest, I swear it to you."

Roarke wasn't certain he believed that, but for now it would be enough. "Fine," he ground out through clenched teeth. "I will do as you ask. I will look into the activities of the dowager."

"Excellent," Thomas said with a smug expression. "You will find her on Kent's Row. At least she knew enough to deposit herself there with the other dried-up crones."

Roarke sighed. First the woman was a flagrant whore with a siren's beauty, now a dried-up crone. It seemed there was no consistency here except for their hatred of the woman. Which meant he had to be extra careful in any of his own judgements of her.

That was the least he could do under the circumstances.

CHAPTER 2

Flora crossed the parlor, teapot in hand, and smiled as she freshened the cups of Valaria, the Dowager Duchess of Gooding, and Bernadette, the Dowager Duchess of Tunbridge. She had known both women for some time, Bernadette since she had come to Kent's Row and joined the widowed duchesses who had made themselves somewhat of a conclave, and Valaria for about six months.

They were her dearest friends and she felt so incredibly lucky to have them in her life.

"The necklace Callum bought you is gorgeous," Bernadette said, and reached out to finger the beautiful sapphire that rested against Valaria's skin. "He does spoil you."

Valaria all but glowed, and it was wonderful to see. She had been so closed off when she arrived on the Row months ago, just after the death of her abusive husband. She had been opposed to the idea that she could ever risk love, but Callum, the Duke of Blackvale, had earned her trust and her heart. Until the end of her official mourning period, though, they could not be public with their engagement. Not that it stopped them from outwardly showing their affection amongst friends.

"He does," Valaria said with an even deeper blush. "I never could have imagined this, but it is better than any dream I ever had. To find someone who so entirely understands me is..." She cut off with a gasp of breath and the brightness of happy tears in her eyes.

As Bernadette leaned over to hug their friend, Flora retook her seat and smoothed her skirts, carefully keeping a warm smile on her face. She didn't want her two friends to see the darker emotions that Valaria's joy brought and ruin their day. She, too, remembered the bliss of having a solid and steadfast partner at her side. She missed that kind of easy happiness that she had felt during her marriage. And she hated herself for being even the tiniest bit jealous of Valaria's glowing future.

"That is enough of my foolishness," Valaria said, laughing as she wiped a few tears from her cheeks. "Honestly, you must get sick of me waxing poetic about how content I am."

"Never!" Bernadette declared without hesitation, and Flora nodded her agreement as she shoved all those harder emotions aside.

"You deserve all your happiness and all that will come in your life," Flora agreed, and meant those words wholeheartedly.

"Well, I thank you. And I know we wouldn't have reached this point without your support," Valaria said. "I shall tell that to everyone I meet that once I can be free to go out again. Just two more months!"

"I cannot wait," Flora said. "I always feel so dreadful when Bernadette and I go out to parties or teas and have to leave you behind."

"Not always alone, though," Bernadette said with a little knowing look.

Valaria ignored the teasing about Callum sneaking into her house to see her regularly and sipped her tea before she said, "So what are your plans tonight?"

"There is a ball," Bernadette said.

Flora jerked her gaze toward their friend, who was suddenly

worrying a thread on the sleeve of her gown, her dark eyes turned down. "And who is hosting the ball?" she encouraged.

Bernadette glared at her, though there was no real anger or heat to the expression. "Oh, stop."

"No, tell her." Flora folded her arms.

"I'm sure I can guess," Valaria said with a laugh. "If Flora is making such a fuss and Bernadette cannot make eye contact, then it can be only one man who is holding the ball, and that is the Duke of Lightmorrow."

Bernadette made a little sound of frustration in her throat and turned away from them a fraction.

"Yes. *Theo* is hosting the ball," Flora said in a little sing-song voice as she drew out the duke's given name. "And Bernadette and I received the same invitation a few days ago, but do you know whose had a special little note scrawled across it?"

Valaria straightened. "What did it say, Bernadette?"

Bernadette pursed her lips and ground out, *"I hope you come, Etta. Theo."*

"You see," Flora said with an arch of her brow. "The man is fascinated by you."

Bernadette pushed to her feet and paced away. "You two are daft! I know the duke from childhood—we are old acquaintances, that is all. There is no way he would ever possibly want me when he could have, and gossip says he has had, practically any other woman in this country. Goodness, you two need a hobby."

She stomped off to get another biscuit and Flora exchanged a brief look with Valaria. They could both see what Bernadette refused to acknowledge. And though Flora had every intention of pushing and helping what could be a happy union along, she did appreciate the anticipation. Another thing she had missed in her life.

Another thing she feared she'd never see again. It had been almost three years since her own husband's death—there was only a month before that sad anniversary. Still, she had long been free to pursue or be pursued, yet there had been no attracted parties, or at least none that turned her head. No flutter of desire. No hint of interest.

Perhaps there never would be. Perhaps hers was a once-in-a-lifetime love and that was all there would be.

"Don't look so troubled," Valaria whispered as she squeezed Flora's hand. "You know Bernadette pretends half her upset when it comes to Theo."

"Oh, I know," Flora said, bringing herself back to the present. "And don't think for one moment that I won't push our girl a little closer to the man if I have any chance to do so."

"I can hear you, you know!" Bernadette said as she pivoted from the sideboard and returned to their circle, a plate of biscuits in hand. "You two are menaces."

"And you love us for it," Flora insisted as she wrapped an arm around Bernadette and squeezed her. "But we won't tease you anymore."

"Wouldn't that be a change," Bernadette muttered, though not darkly. "Please, let's talk about any other subject. The weather, the roads, the fact that you look so ridiculously pretty in that dress, Flora. Anything but this."

The women laughed and then surrendered to their friend's desire, changing the subject to other matters than the men in their lives…or lack thereof. And Flora was able to push down those dark thoughts, those lonely resentments until they only became twinges of something ugly.

And she hoped, as she had been hoping for some time, that one day she would be able to accept what was and not long for what had been. Or worse, what might not ever be again.

Roarke stood in the doorway of his mother's desperately small home and frowned at the disrepair he saw. Now that the two hundred fifty pounds he'd been promised had been received, he would have to have someone come look at the crack in the mantelpiece and the loose window. It would be cold soon—he didn't want his mother to suffer.

He smiled sadly as her carer, Hilde Smith, tucked a blanket around her legs. "There now, Mrs. Desmond," Hilde said gently. "Are you going to say good day to your son?"

"I don't have a son," his mother said weakly, and her brow knitted with confusion.

Roarke tried to ignore how those words cut. She didn't say them to be cruel. She just sometimes didn't recall him. He stepped forward, took a seat across from her and smiled at her. "It's me, Mama, do you remember?"

There was a hint of recognition there and she blinked. "Oh…yes. I suppose I do."

He took her hand and they talked for a few moments, of nothing of importance. He couldn't tell her things anymore, not like he had as a boy when she was light and fun. He had to be careful now, speak of bland topics like the weather so that she didn't get confused or upset.

Eventually, she began to look tired and he lifted her hand to his lips, kissing her knuckles gently. "You rest now, Mama. I'm just going to talk to Mrs. Smith for a moment."

She didn't answer, just stared into the fire and he sighed as he got up and Hilde followed him to the tiny foyer. They held stares for a moment. Hilde had been helping his mother since even before his father's death. She was kind and patient, everything one would want for his mother.

"I'll have the window fixed," he promised softly. "Is there anything else you need?"

She shifted with discomfort. "I-I care about your mother, sir. You know that."

He nodded, even as dread lifted in his chest. "I do know. And I know that you help her at a reduced rate. That it isn't fair."

"I realize it's all you can do," she said. "But you know I have a son of my own. He hasn't been able to get much work as of late and he's struggling. I don't know if I can...if I can continue, as much as I want to be there for you mother."

He shut his eyes and tried to quell the flare of panic in his chest. "I am terribly sorry, Hilde. I know you could likely find another position that would pay better. I'm...I'm working on something that would allow me to offer you more this year to stay. I can give you twenty more now and I'm hoping I would be able to increase your weekly wage by a pound after I compete this...this duty."

He flinched as he said it. That duty felt so filthy to him. To spy on some woman he didn't even know and report back. But when he looked at his mother, now dozing in her chair, he knew he had no choice.

Hilde nodded. "That would be a great help, sir."

"I'll have the twenty delivered tomorrow by the latest, and let you know when they'll come to fix the window. And I'll deliver on the rest as soon as possible."

She hesitated before she briefly touched his hand. "I know you're doing the best you can, sir. Please don't be too hard on yourself."

"I think I must be, Hilde. But I appreciate you. Good day."

He stepped out and took the reins of his horse, who he had tied on the post by the front door of his mother's...well, he supposed he had to call it a hovel, didn't he? And it would get no better if he didn't do as he'd been told by his horrible cousins.

"Time to pay the piper," he muttered, and swung up to ride to his club. He had continued to pay the dues there, hating that little pleasure but also knowing that his connections in the place might provide him with some opportunities. And today he needed to seek one out.

When he arrived, he went in, greeting the man at the door. Once inside, he looked around, trying to find a face who might help him in this devil's errand. At last he settled on one man and drew a deep breath before he came across the floor.

"Lightmorrow?" he said, as casually as he could be as he approached the handsome duke seated by the window, reading a newspaper.

Lightmorrow looked up, staring at Roarke like he didn't know him, and his heart sank. But before he could explain himself, Lightmorrow pushed to his feet. "Great God, Desmond, I didn't recognize you for a moment."

Roarke extended a hand and the men shook. "No reason to—I don't think we've seen each other since I left Eton all those years ago. At least not in anything more than passing."

He did not add that he'd avoided Lightmorrow and his ilk on purpose, out of humiliation for the fact that his father had lost whatever small fortune he had, which resulted in Roarke's being plucked from the best schools and dropped into a very different world.

"Yes. Please sit." Lightmorrow motioned to the chair across from the one he had been seated in. "How have you been?"

They chatted for a while, Roarke's anxiety mounting in his chest. He needed to find a way to connect to someone who might get him closer to the Dowager Duchess of Sidmouth, but he had no idea if Lightmorrow even knew the lady. Even though Lightmorrow's reputation would imply that he would. The man liked widows, everyone knew that.

"You know I'm having a gathering tonight," Lightmorrow said, and Roarke perked up.

"Oh, are you?"

"Yes. I'd love to have you come and catch up. It sounds as though you could use the entertainment."

Roarke forced a smile. "Only if there will be a few eligible ladies in attendance."

Lightmorrow's laughter filled the room. "It's me, Desmond. Of course there will be eligible ladies. It only depends if you're looking for fun or for something more serious."

Roarke shrugged. "I suppose either will do."

"Well, I can tell you that there will be quite a few unmarried misses who are sniffing out a future, as well as a handful of widows, including several who are looking for lovers."

Stomach turning, Roarke swallowed hard and thought of his mother, her carer ready to depart for lack of funds that he could provide by just playing the bastard for a little while.

"Would one of those widows be the Duchess of Sidmouth?" He hesitated as he waited to see if Lightmorrow might link him to his late uncle. After all, he shared a last name with the man's first wife. But there was no flicker of recognition, just surprise.

"She will be there," Lightmorrow said. "What do you know of the duchess?"

"I've heard she is uncommonly beautiful," Roarke said. "Someone told me that."

Lightmorrow nodded slowly. "Indeed, the lady is lovely. And she has been alone for a while. I could make the introduction if you are interested in making her acquaintance."

Relief flooded Roarke, along with regret. He had chosen Lightmorrow to approach because of his string of past lovers who were also widows, and it seemed the universe was guiding him to perform his wicked duty. "That would be wonderful."

"Do you know where my townhouse is here in London?" Lightmorrow asked. "Guests will begin to arrive at nine."

"I do and I will be there." Roarke stood and held out his hand again. "Now I must go if I'm to take care of everything on my list before I join you tonight."

"I look forward to seeing you there," Lightmorrow said, now watching him with a more appraising eye. "It was nice to see you today."

"You as well. I'll speak to you this evening."

Roarke left then, hating himself for what he would have to do. But as had often been the case in his life, there was no choice.

CHAPTER 3

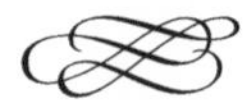

By the time Roarke stood in Lightmorrow's ballroom a few hours after their encounter at the club, he had managed to convince himself that he wasn't the actual worst person in the country. He wasn't going to hurt the duchess, after all. Just ascertain if she was doing something his cousins would consider untoward. If they used some kind of legal means to deny her an additional ten thousand pounds of inheritance, well, the lady had a fine sum that had already been delivered to her years before.

So he stood with Lightmorrow, after his arrival, watching the increasingly crowded ball, and tried to steady himself. At least the company wasn't terrible so far. Lightmorrow was proving himself to be amusing and intelligent, despite his reputation with the ladies that could make even the most profligate rake blush a little.

"Do you know Grayson Danford?" Lightmorrow said over the fray.

Roarke's eyes went wide as he turned toward his old friend. "I...I have heard of him. He made his fortune in canals, yes?"

"He did," Lightmorrow said. "And he's working on something new. Steam, I think he said. Something about steam engines? He's far too intelligent for me to pay attention. But you used to like that sort of forward thinking, if I recall, so perhaps you two will get along. He's coming over now."

He motioned toward a tall, hard-faced gentleman who was nearly at their side, and Roarke stood up straighter as Danford reached them and greeted their host. Then Lightmorrow made the further introductions, and for a moment they all talked about the most surface of topics.

"I know you think me quite daft," Lightmorrow said after a moment. "But I think you'll find a fellow inventive mind in our friend Desmond here. He likes the idea of steam engines, as well.

Danford speared Roarke with an interested stare, his dark eyes bright with excitement. "*That* is where the real future is."

Roarke lifted his brows. "I happen to agree."

Danford's gaze flitted over him, reading him in an instant. "Yes, I seem to recall you invested with Harrimon, wasn't it?"

"Disastrously," Roarke said, and hated the humiliation that flooded him. "Lost everything, I fear."

"Well, he had the wrong method. It's the rail that will lead the future." Danford sounded so certain it was difficult not to believe him. "I'm putting together a group of men willing to bet on that very outcome. You ought to consider buying in. I guarantee nothing, of course, but the return could be very high."

Roarke shifted. Everyone knew that when Danford talked, it was best to listen. And he so desperately wanted to say yes. Only he couldn't. At present, after he paid his mother's expenses and the lowly overhead he kept for himself, he had approximately one hundred pounds to his name and it would have to last him until his next handout from his cousins. Certainly Danford would expect far more expenditure to be part of his project.

"I'll have to consider it," Roarke said.

Lightmorrow laughed. "Well, now I've done my most boring duty as a host and let you talk business. But now you must pay attention to all the loveliness to behold all around you."

He motioned to the ladies in the room around them, and

Danford smiled as he looked across the crowd toward a lovely woman with dark hair and startling gray-blue eyes. His wife, Roarke thought he recalled. Danford's normally hard and intense expression softened. "You may be right, Lightmorrow. Perhaps it's time to step away from business. I shall ask my wife." He faced Roarke briefly. "Reach out to my offices if you have an interest. I'm always looking for men with an eye to the future. Good evening."

He tipped his head and then slipped away into the crowd toward the lady. Lightmorrow shook his head. "Besotted," he grumbled. "Every one of my friends has been similarly struck, it seems. You and I must focus on remaining—"

He didn't finish the sentence but instead stared off toward the entrance to the ballroom. Roarke followed his gaze and caught his own breath. Two women had entered the room. One was a slender, dark-haired woman with a shy blush to her cheeks. The other was petite and curvaceous, her auburn hair done stylishly at the nape of an infinitely kissable neck.

He blinked. "Who is that?"

"Etta," Lightmorrow said softly and then shook his head. "Forgive me, the Duchess of Tunbridge. And the shorter lady with her is the focus of your questions earlier. The Duchess of Sidmouth."

Roarke's eyes went wide as he looked again at the two ladies who were now moving across the room, smiling at friends. *That* was his uncle's second wife? That absolute stunning vision of a woman who looked like she could still claim her spot as debutante was the much-hated Flora? No wonder his cousins had despised her. She was a breath of fresh air, a spot of light one couldn't look away from.

And far, far too young for his uncle, who had married her when he was into his fifties. Arranged marriage or not, it was unseemly. She would have married him when she was barely into her twenties, if that. Was it possible his cousins were right in their assessment of her? Had this vision used her stunning beauty against the old man, manipulating herself into a fortune?

The ladies were now feet away and Roarke noticed that some of the color had drained from Lightmorrow's face. Like he was just as enthralled as Roarke was. He found himself tensing as he awaited the exchange between the handsome duke and the stunning dowager.

But when Lightmorrow spoke, it wasn't to her. Instead he reached out two hands and caught the other lady's. "Etta," he said softly. "Aren't you lovely."

The Duchess of Tunbridge blushed to the roots of her hair. "You are a tease," she admonished shakily. "What a party, Theo. A success, as always."

The Duchess of Sidmouth cleared her throat playfully. "Yes, and I'm here, too."

Lightmorrow shook his head and leaned forward to clasp her hand, lifting it to his lips with distraction. "Of course. Welcome to you both. Forgive my manners, let me introduce you to an old friend from my school days, Mr. Roarke Desmond. Desmond, these are the Duchesses of Tunbridge and Sidmouth."

The Duchess of Tunbridge glanced at him briefly before her attention was drawn back to Lightmorrow, but Flora…that was her given name, wasn't it? And it fit, for she looked as beautiful as nature, herself. Flora let her gaze flit over him briefly. "Good evening, Mr. Desmond. How nice it is to meet you."

She might have said some more pleasantries and he would have responded, but the Duchess of Tunbridge leaned in. "Lightmorrow has asked me to dance. Excuse me, Flora."

Flora smiled after her and Lightmorrow as they departed, leaving Roarke alone with her. He stepped a little closer so they could talk and got the lightest whiff of rose petals on her skin. Intoxicating.

She glanced up at him and smiled, a very genuine and warm expression. "So you knew Lightmorrow when he was a recalcitrant youth, did you?"

He chuckled at her question. "Indeed. A rapscallion he was, even then. Always getting himself into one scrape or another and bringing the lot of us along with him."

"How old were you when you met?" she asked.

"Twelve," he said. "And we remained school chums for several years until I—" He cut himself off.

She laughed a little, a husky sound. "Bernadette, that is the Duchess of Tunbridge, is also an old friend of his."

He looked across the room to where Lightmorrow was turning around the dancefloor with the duchess in his arms. They were not talking, but they did look at each other with a great deal of focus. "Hmmm, they do seem like…friends."

She let out a little snort that told him she saw the connection between their companions just as he did. He looked at her from the corner of his eye. "So, the Duchess of Sidmouth," he said carefully. "And where is the duke?"

He asked the question to judge her reaction, but also because he wished to see if she had recognized his last name as one associated with her late husband's first wife.

She bent her head and took the shallowest of breaths. "Er, my husband passed nearly three years ago, Mr. Desmond."

He heard the faint strain to her tone, but couldn't place the reason. Sadness? Or frustration? Relief?

"My apologies," he said swiftly. "A woman of your years and beauty, I assumed you must be married to the current duke."

She pulled a face that she swiftly hid. It seemed the lady felt no more affection toward her stepchildren than they felt toward her. "Er, no. I believe the current duke is unmarried as of yet. We are not close since his father's death. I'm not up on family news."

"Ah," he said, and shrugged. "I'm afraid I'm also not much up on the news of those of such rank. I run in quite different circles normally." He nodded toward Lightmorrow. "Present friends aside, of course."

"You don't miss much," she said softly, and for the first time he noted a hint of bitterness to her tone, even though it was in no way reflected on her face. She still looked serene and utterly lovely as she looked out over the crowd.

"Perhaps not," he said. He turned more fully toward her and she glanced over at him. Her gaze lingered on his face for a moment, and then she caught a little breath and ducked it away.

Before he could say anything else, she took a step back. "Er, well, it's been a pleasure to make your acquaintance, Mr. Desmond. It looks as though Bernadette has finished her dance with the duke and I should join her. I wish you a fine evening."

He bit his tongue to keep himself from calling her back to him and instead merely inclined his head. "Your Grace."

She pivoted then and darted off into the crowd. He sighed as he watched her go. The few moments spent with her had not revealed her to be a monster, which would have certainly made his life easier. He could have reported back to his cousins, called his duties complete and collected a tidy sum of blunt.

Instead he'd been left with the uneasy attraction to a woman he certainly should have no interest in. And a feeling that when she walked away it was the first time he could draw a first breath since they had been introduced.

"Bollocks," he muttered beneath his breath before he turned and made his own way into the crowd away from where she had gone.

Flora found herself glancing across the crowded ballroom for what had to have been the tenth time that long night. She knew what she was searching for, even if she might not have ever admitted it to anyone else. And when her gaze fell on Mr. Roarke Desmond, her ridiculous heart throbbed just the tiniest bit faster.

Of course, admit it or not, she had clearly made herself too plain, for Bernadette made a little snort at her side. "He's a handsome gentleman."

Flora tore her eyes from him and speared her friend with what she hoped was a reasonably innocent expression. "Who?"

Bernadette pursed her lips. "Mister...what was his name?"

"Desmond," Flora said, and then blushed as she realized she'd just proven Bernadette's point. "Ugh, you are terrible."

Bernadette shrugged. "I don't see what the problem is. You don't have to hide it if you feel a little regard for a person."

"I don't *feel* anything," Flora said with a shake of her head as she stole another glance at him. "I met the man all of two hours ago and we talked for less than five minutes. I'm looking. There is no harm in looking."

"I agree," Bernadette said, this time a little softer, and when Flora glanced at her she realized her friend was staring at Lightmorrow, who was now laughing with Valaria's secret fiancé, Callum. Bernadette must have felt Flora looking because she tore her gaze away and refocused it on Flora. "And *you* could do more than look if you are of a mind, you know."

Flora tried to think of a witty rejoinder at that statement, but her hands had begun to shake and she felt the color go out of her cheeks.

Bernadette made a soft sound in her throat and stepped closer. "Oh dearest, I apologized. I should not have teased. I know what a struggle it's been for you these past few years."

Flora sighed. "I'm in the odd position that I actually both loved and *liked* my husband. Very different from a great many merry widows who are ready to pounce on their next conquest before the grave is even fully covered by dirt." She caught her breath. "I don't mean Valaria, of course."

"Of course not," Bernadette reassured her. "Valaria was in a very different situation—no one could blame her for celebrating her husband's death rather than grieving it. But this is not an all or nothing situation, is it? You can have loved Stuart and miss him, but not lock yourself away forever as if you died alongside him. You have money and freedom, you could seek a new husband if you wished. Or...or a lover."

Bernadette blushed as she said it, and Flora couldn't help but do the same, especially when she glanced at Mr. Desmond again and found him watching her with unmistakable interest in his expression. When was the last time she'd felt that kind of regard? When was the last time it had elicited a stir of reaction in her stomach when she had?

She shook her head. "This is all rather silly a conversation, isn't it? Whether or not I found someone here tonight to be a handsome gentleman, whether or not I intend to open my future up to the possibility of a connection to another man, there is not much chance I'll ever see Mr. Desmond again. So I needn't worry about him, even if I do promise to consider your very good advice about my potential future."

Bernadette glanced over her shoulder at Mr. Desmond again and then wrapped her arm around Flora. "Whatever you wish."

Flora elbowed her gently. "Now, do you want to talk about that intense dance you shared with Lightmorrow earlier tonight?"

Bernadette threw up her hands. "Great God, but you and Valaria are singular. No, I don't want to discuss it. I want to go have some watered-down punch and giggle like debutantes about Lady Beasley's ghastly hat."

Flora smiled as they moved together toward the refreshment table at the back of the room. "Very well. That sounds perfect."

And it did. Almost. But even though she would not speak about Roarke Desmond again that night, she feared she wouldn't be able to dismiss the stirring in her body that the handsome man had created.

CHAPTER 4

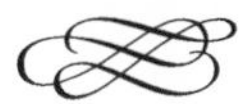

It had been three days since Roarke's encounter with Flora at Lightmorrow's ball, but she had rarely left his mind since that night. He told himself it was because he was doing his due diligence on the matter. Research into her habits and the company she kept, casual rides past her home on Kent's Row to get an understanding of her circumstances. Discreetly following her if she went out shopping or to visit with friends.

And yes, he was determining a pattern in his research, there was no denying it. But there was also no denying that he also found himself increasingly interested in the lady. She was...kind. That was the overwhelming impression he got from anyone who agreed to speak about her. She was kind to those around her, regardless of their rank and circumstances.

That was rare enough in itself.

And as for his research project, he had seen no hint of a man in her life. There was no rumor of men either. To his great pleasure, even if he shouldn't have felt such a reaction. His cousins would be livid, he knew.

He was sitting in the park across from her home now, watching the door to her house. She came out every day at the same time, strolled the park by herself, without even a maid in attendance. That had startled him enough the first time he saw her do so that he had followed at a short distance to see if she was, indeed, meeting someone. And if not, that she remained safe while she roamed alone.

Now she entered the park, a serene expression on that lovely face, and something came over him. Something foolish. He stepped out where she could see him and called out, "Your Grace?"

She stopped in the path and turned toward his voice. He saw color enter her cheeks as she saw him, but then she stepped toward him. "Goodness, Mr. Desmond, what a surprise!"

He smiled as he met her on the path, a hand outstretched to shake hers. When she touched him, a flutter of electric heat seemed to follow. "Your Grace," he said. "What are you doing here?"

"I-I live just there," she said, motioning to the colorful row of houses beyond the park. "On Kent's Row."

"Ah," he said. "And I was calling on a friend on the other side of the park and thought to take a walk before I went on my way. What a wonderful surprise. Would you...would you like to walk together? Or is that too presumptuous in an acquaintance so young as ours?"

That blush on her cheeks deepened and she dipped her head. "Er, no. Not at all. I would very much enjoy a walk together. Please, lead the way."

He did so, stepping onto the path as she fell in beside him. For a few moments the air between them was silent. Too silent. He cleared his throat. "Kent's Row. Why have I heard of that name before?" he asked, pretending he didn't already know everything about the place.

A slight smile tilted her lips. "Perhaps because it is a place to put duchesses out to pasture?"

He blinked at her forthright response. "Goodness, that sounds dire! Certainly that cannot be true."

"And yet it is," she said with a laugh. "My neighbors are lovely, but mostly they are much older dowagers whose sons and even grandsons have taken over the titles their husbands once held."

"I see. You must be lonely there, without neighbors your age to meet with." He glanced at her from the corner of his eye, watching to see if there anything in her face hinting that she kept some kind of secret male company.

But she shook her head and didn't look reserved on the subject. "Not at all. The older ladies are fine company. And my neighbors on either side are Valaria—she is the Duchess of Gooding and still in mourning—and of course Bernadette, the Duchess of Tunbridge, who you met at the ball a few days ago. We're all young widows."

"And all chose such a place to reside," he said. "Not that it is any of my business, it just seems peculiar that such a vivacious person would lock herself away thus."

Flora turned toward him. "And how have you determined I am vivacious?" she said with a playful smile. "Was it my scintillating conversation about your friendship with Lightmorrow at the ball?"

"You were a charming, albeit brief, companion. But one couldn't look at you and not see your sparkle, Your Grace."

The teasing in her demeanor changed and she shifted as if his compliment made her uncomfortable. She stepped back. "That is kindly said." She stared off toward the row of homes behind them and let out her breath in the slightest of sighs. "I cannot speak for my friends, or I will not at any rate, but I definitely wasn't forced into my life on the Row. I simply did not think I'd ever live as anything but a staid dowager ever again. So why not retire to a place where I could easily be just that?"

He wrinkled his brow at that, yet again, direct answer. A staid dowager didn't sound like the kind of woman who was harboring a secret lover or undercover life as her stepchildren had implied.

"And so you...*embroider*?" he asked.

She laughed. "Oh, your tone makes that sound so grandmotherly. I'll have you know I have a great deal of talent when it comes to embroidery!"

"I would not doubt it," he said, raising his hands in playful surrender.

"Besides, some of the best parties are held by staid dowagers, aren't they? I do not wish to brag, but I am well known for my entertaining fetes amongst my friends." She folded her arms and then her expression faltered a bit. "Perhaps...perhaps you would like to join us in a few days' time."

He blinked. "You're inviting me to a party?"

"A gathering of friends. You already know Lightmorrow, and I saw you talking to Callum...er, Blackvale at Lightmorrow's ball, so I think you must know him, as well. You all went to school together, yes?"

There was a brief sour reaction in his chest to the lady's use of Blackvale's first name. He couldn't imagine her matching well with serious Blackvale, who he did know a bit from childhood, though not as well as Lightmorrow. But the two dukes were friends—one could not be acquainted with one without the other, it seemed. He liked Blackvale, though he'd found the man to be distracted and a little secretive at the party a few days ago. Lightmorrow had teased him about secret assignations.

And Roarke's heart sank. Had he stumbled across the truth about Flora? Was she covertly meeting with Blackvale?

"I would very much like to attend," he said, a little more flatly than he might have said prior to this question about her association with his friend. "You may get my direction from Lightmorrow, if you like, and send me the details."

"I shall do so," she said.

She looked as though she might say more, and he stepped away to prevent it, now feeling uncertain again and not liking that his mood was so tied to a lady he didn't even know and was acting covertly against.

"And now I shall leave you to your walk," he said, breaking eye contact. "I look forward to seeing you in a few days."

With that he tipped his head and strode away, hearing her soft, confusion-laced "Good afternoon" echo behind him on the breeze. He shook his head as he exited the park and forced himself not to look back at her. If he was going to act on his awful cousins' behalf, he needed to get his head straight. He most definitely didn't need to get the fact that he found this woman wildly attractive become intermixed with whatever distasteful investigation he was conducting. That was the way to heartache.

When Flora stepped into her foyer half an hour later, she was trying to convince herself she wasn't still stinging from the dismissive way Mr. Desmond had left her in the park earlier. She'd been surprised so see him there, his longish dark hair catching on the breeze and his sharp green eyes moving over her with what had certainly felt like interest.

Until it wasn't. Until he'd gone cool and left her. Had she done something wrong? It had been so long since anyone paid her attention, she felt awkward with any focused on her now. Perhaps she'd said something or done something that…

She stopped in the foyer with a frown. Goodness, she had no interest in any man—why was she so focused on this one just because he was so very handsome?

"Your Grace?"

She started as she realized her butler was standing at her side, hand outstretched for her bonnet. She removed it. "I beg your pardon, Hendricks. I'm obviously woolgathering."

"Of course, madam. The Duchess of Gooding is in the parlor with tea. I believe she knew you might be back from your walk around this time and I didn't think you would mind the intrusion."

Flora shifted. Her habits were often predicable, so she was sure Valaria would make a comment on the fact that she was ten minutes later than normal in her return from her walk. Probably because she'd been analyzing every interaction with Roarke...with Mr. Desmond.

"I'll join her," she forced herself to say as she made her way to the parlor. She drew a deep breath before she entered, and hoped Valaria wouldn't see the upset that felt so plain on her face.

"Flora," Valaria said with a smile as she crossed the room to press a kiss to Flora's cheek. "Don't you look fresh faced from your walk? I so respect that you always take time for a stroll alone every day. I asked Hendricks for tea—I hope you don't mind."

"Of course not. Shall I pour?"

"I already did," Valaria said, and moved to fetch the perfectly prepared cup of tea from the sideboard. They moved to the settee and sat together, and it was only then that Valaria leaned in and her brow wrinkled. "What's wrong?"

Flora shook her head with a small, humorless laugh. "You know everyone talks about the benefits of having true friends, but no one talks about the downsides."

"The downsides?" Valaria asked. "What do you mean?"

"That you and Bernadette always see through me, just as I have learned to see through you. It is mightily annoying on certain days, I will tell you." Flora set her cup down. "We could play a game where I tell you nothing is wrong and then you'll push and then I'll tell you a little lie to throw you off and then you'll catch me at it and eventually I'll capitulate and tell you everything."

"That would fill the afternoon, it seems," Valaria said, eyes both filled with humor and concern. She leaned a little closer and touched Flora's hand. "Dearest, if there is anyone who understands not wanting to tell every secret, it's me."

Flora let out her breath. Valaria had kept a terrible secret for weeks upon her arrival to the Row. Certainly Flora's confusing exchange with a handsome man was nothing in comparison.

But Valaria continued, "I want to help you if I can. But if you want to claim your right to privacy until you are ready, I won't push. We'll talk about fall leaves and the exhibit of portraits by Ezra Pembroke at the Royal Academy. It just opened, you know."

Flora hesitated. Valaria would be true to her word and they could discuss these surface topics. But did she want that?

When she was silent for a moment, Valaria tilted her head. "Or perhaps we could talk about the handsome gentleman who caught you attention at Lightmorrow's ball a few days ago."

Flora worried her hands before her. "Bernadette reported all to you?"

"Of course," Valaria said with a laugh. "She said his name was…Desmond?"

"Roarke Desmond," Flora said. "A friend of Lightmorrow's from school, and seemingly Callum's, as well." Valaria's cheeks brightened a little and Flora narrowed her gaze. "Though judging from that expression, it seems you already know that. Were you talking to your future husband about him? About me?"

"I had to vet him on your behalf," Valaria said with a shake of her head.

"Oh, Valaria." Flora got up. "That is silly. Yes, I met the man at the ball and he is very handsome. I'm a widow—I'm not in the ground myself. I noticed his looks, just like some young debutante might have. And yes, when I bumped into him in the park, I enjoyed his company. But it seems to be for nothing because he left me soon after."

Valaria stared at her in confusion. "The park? What are you talking about?"

"I saw him when I was out on my walk a while ago." Flora shook her head.

"Ah!" Valaria's eyes lit up. "And how was it?"

Flora worried her lip. "I-I invited him to our little gathering on Friday night."

"To our gathering," Valaria repeated. "Oh."

"I don't know what came over me. I know it's usually just the three of us friends, plus Callum and Lightmorrow. I should have asked you first. You and Callum are in no way public with your relationship."

Valaria shrugged. "Honestly, Callum spoke highly of the man when we discussed him after the ball. He says there is much to respect about him. Apparently he takes care of his ailing mother."

"Oh," Flora said softly. Well, that was a point in the man's favor, cool attitude or not.

Valaria continued, "And it's only little while more before the truth comes out about my engagement. I suppose there would be no harm in allowing one more friend to know about us." As Flora sighed in relief that she hadn't betrayed her friend in her haste to be closer to a man she didn't even know that well, Valaria caught her hand. "I think the bigger question is *why* did you invite him?"

Flora caught her breath as she thought of Roarke's green gaze holding on her face as he smiled and made her heart flutter. "I just thought…I thought that he knew Callum and Theo and he might fit."

Valaria stared. "So you weren't thinking of yourself at all then?"

"N-No," Flora lied. She paced away to the window and stared out at the very park where she'd walked with the man. The spot where he'd excused himself, and she blushed all over again. "You are happy, Valaria, and I am happy for you. And I think if you and I do a little pushing, Bernadette could also be happy."

"I assume you are talking about her feelings for Theo."

Flora turned back. "Yes."

"I agree they would be well-matched if they could manage to hoist themselves over each other's walls. But we're not talking about my life with Callum—that is happily resolved. We're not talking about Theo and Bernadette—that is a work in progress, a longer-term project. My dear, we are talking about *you*."

"I loved my husband," Flora said wistfully.

Valaria got up and now she looked uncomfortable. "You say that, but…"

Flora drew back. "Do you doubt me?" Her heart throbbed in her chest and upset lifted, but it was more directed at herself than her friend. After all, her memories of Stuart, her feelings for him...they were fading over time.

"No, not at all," Valaria said. "I *know* you loved him. The warmth in your voice when you talk about him is so genuine. But I also know your age difference was vast. And judging from what we've discussed, the relationship between you wasn't overly...passionate."

Flora felt the flame of humiliation heat her cheeks at that delicate subject. "I-I...just because you and Callum can't bear to not touch each other for more than ten minutes put together doesn't mean that's everyone's path. Stuart was older. We were loving companions and connected friends. He was my whole world for a time." Now the tears stung and she welcomed them, because they made her feel like she hadn't forgotten him after all. "Perhaps not everyone was made for a great passion."

Valaria took her hands and squeezed gently. "Perhaps that is true. I didn't mean to upset you, and I apologize that I did. But you must know that I adore you. And I'd love to see you find a second life, a second wind. You are still young. And you have freedoms that you were not afforded before your first marriage. So if you do not find some great new love, you might still be able to have some fun."

"Perhaps," Flora said. "I don't think I'd ever considered it before now. But handsome or not, Roarke...Mr. Desmond might not be the man to pursue such things with. After all, we were talking in the park and then I must have bored him because he excused himself rather suddenly."

Valaria pursed her lips. "Well, if any man could be bored by you, he doesn't deserve you."

"You look like you're ready to go to battle with him," Flora laughed.

"I will if you'd like. Take up my sword and smite him for not appreciating you!"

"I adore you for that," Flora said, and wrapped and arm around her friend. "But perhaps it's for the best. I can admire his handsome visage from afar and not be too pressured in any other way. And now we've discussed this far too much. Let's talk about the wedding plans. Have you decided how you two will announce your engagement once your official mourning period is over and how long you will wait until you wed?"

Valaria's eyes lit up and she didn't hesitate as she began to wax poetic about her future. Flora couldn't help but be warmed by her friends' happy glow. Still, she also thought about Valaria's comments that she, herself, should consider a second act in her life. She just didn't know if she could move on, let alone if she wanted to.

But when she thought of Roarke Desmond's intense green eyes, she still felt butterflies.

CHAPTER 5

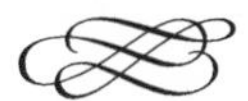

Roarke had less than a minute from the time he handed over the reins of his horse to when the door to Flora's house opened. One minute to calm his expression and try to manage his pounding heart. He was not here because he found the lady attractive or interesting. He was here to put an end once and for all the investigation his cousins demanded of him and collect the other half of the money he would earn for doing so. Tonight he would determine decisively that she had no lovers or secret relationships.

He only wished that didn't make him feel like the worst kind of arse. Even thoughts of his mother and her needs couldn't change that.

The minute passed and the door opened. A stern-faced butler nodded as Roarke gave his name and handed over his coat and hat. "They are gathered in the parlor, sir," the man intoned as he led Roarke down the hall.

He heard voices as they neared the room. Laughter and chatter of several people at once. When Flora had sent the information to him after their meeting in the park a few days earlier, she had not given much detail. Just the time of the meeting and the date. Now he wondered how many people would be gathered there and if he would have time for his investigation, after all.

The door opened and he stepped inside, hardly hearing as the butler announced his name. The room as a whole turned and he realized it was only five others gathered there. Lightmorrow, of course, he knew. The duke was standing next to the Duchess of Tunbridge, who Roarke had met at the ball a week before.

Next was the Duke of Blackvale, who Roarke had also gone to school with. The lady who had her arm linked with his he didn't recognize. She was very pretty, with dark brown hair and gray-blue eyes. The fact that it wasn't Flora he was attending gave Roarke a thrill he didn't particularly care for. That wasn't his role. When would he remember that?

And finally there was Flora, herself. She was lovely, always more lovely than he recalled her to be, which had been shocking when he saw her in the park and was no less so now. Her auburn hair was done in in a complicated twisting style that highlighted her face perfectly. She wore a dusky blue gown with translucent layers beautifully folded and tucked over one another.

She all but flowed forward toward him, hand outstretched and eyes bright. "Mr. Desmond, welcome."

He smiled as he took her hand, wishing he could school the throb of his heart when he touched her. "Your Grace. It seems I am late—my apologies."

"Not at all," she assured him, as she withdrew her hand and placed it on her heart almost absently. "I believe you know almost everyone here. I will introduce with first names, as that is our way when we're all together. Too many dukes and duchesses in a room and it becomes a comedy of errors when one Your Grace bleeds into another."

First names. Roarke shivered at the thought of being allowed to call her Flora. Of her saying Roarke. That was intimate, inappropriate in most company. And he longed for it.

"I can imagine," he said. "As long as no one is offended by a lowly non-duke saying their first names."

"As long as you do it with cheek," Lightmorrow said with a laugh.

Flora joined the laughter. "Theo and Callum I think you know."

Roarke inclined his head. He hadn't ever called either man by their first name, but neither seemed offended by the idea. "Gentlemen."

"Roarke," Callum said with a warmth to his smile, like he was giving permission.

Flora continued, "You met Bernadette as the Duchess of Tunbridge at Theo's ball last week. I believe the only stranger to you here is our dear Valaria, the Duchess of Gooding."

Roarke's eyes went wide. He had heard of the death of the Duke of Gooding. Whispers of a violent accident had reached even his ears, but it hadn't seemed too long ago. The lady ought not to have been out of mourning and yet she wore full color in this company, and the way she stroked her fingers along Callum's arm made it clear she was attached to his old schoolmate.

"Your Grace," he said so that his assessment would not be clear.

"Valaria," she reminded him, holding his gaze evenly, almost in challenge.

He didn't intend to rise to the challenge, of course. His duty was not to investigate whether *she* was carousing with a gentlemen before her mourning was over. It was none of his business, and he was happy for Callum, who looked positively besotted by the lovely lady.

And yet it led to more pause about Flora. If her friend could be having a secret relationship kept out of the public eye, Flora might also be capable and he simply hadn't figured it out yet.

He pushed the thought from his mind. "Valaria," he repeated with a smile, and then turned back to Flora.

"And that is our entire party," she said, he thought a little nervously. "As I mentioned, it is a small party. Just friends."

There was something warm that spread throughout his whole chest at the idea that she might see him as a friend. "Then it will be a charming evening."

"Come," Callum said as Valaria slid her arm free of his. "Let Theo and I talk you into a drink before supper."

He motioned to the sideboard, and Theo and Roarke followed him. Meanwhile, the ladies stepped to the other side of the room and bent their heads in what looked like close conversation. By the way Bernadette and Valaria looked at him from time to time, he couldn't help but believe they were discussing him.

"You have passed the test," Callum chuckled as he handed over a whisky.

"The test?" Roarke repeated. "What test is that?"

"The character appraisal of the Duchesses of Kent's Row," Theo said as he took a swig of his own drink. "Or at least the most interesting three of them."

"I will defer to your knowledge," Roarke said. "You two seem to know them all well. I, of course, just met the Duchess…" He faded off and shook his head. Flora was right, it was too complicated to even try for propriety when there were so many Their Graces in the room. "I only met Bernadette and Flora at Lightmorrow's ball."

"Yes, our wonderful Flora," Callum mused. "What do you think of her?"

Now Roarke's brow wrinkled. From Callum's tone, it was clear Roarke didn't just have to pass the judgment of the ladies. He cleared his throat. "She is lovely. And my exchanges with her have been…" So many words flooded his mind. Enchanting, fascinating, intoxicating. "…pleasant."

Theo pulled a face. "Pleasant," he repeated.

"What do you want me to say?" Roarke asked, forcing a chuckle. "As I said, I barely know the lady."

Not entirely true thanks to his research, but he'd rather hear the take of his friends than reveal he was all but stalking the lady on behalf of stepchildren who'd like to destroy her. That would certainly change the tenor of this evening.

"Well, she is a widow, of course," Callum said.

"Yes, that I know," Roarke said. "She was married to the Duke of Sidmouth."

He held his breath at that statement. No one had made the connection between himself and the late first wife of Sidmouth. The first duchess was long dead now, so there was no reason that would change, but he still knew it was possible they would call him on the relation and then this entire endeavor would likely end swiftly.

But neither seemed to make the connection. "Yes," Callum said.

"He was a bit older than she was," Roarke continued, "if I'm remembering correctly."

"Much older." Theo shook his head. "And yet she truly seems to have cared for him."

Roarke straightened. There it was. A glimpse of Flora's inner thoughts on his uncle coming from someone who actually knew her. Who she might be more honest with about the subject if she had, indeed, been as indifferent as his cousin's claimed. "Does she say so?"

"Yes," Callum said slowly, his brow wrinkling. "I'm shocked you sound interested about that particular tidbit. Or is it that you are interested in the lady, herself?"

The world felt like it screeched to a sudden halt at that question and Roarke couldn't help but let his gaze slide toward Flora once more. She was smiling. Laughing. Beautiful and bright.

"That is what the other ladies think, you know," Theo said. "And be forewarned, you might have to walk through some fire to reach her if that's true. They'll stand for each other."

Roarke continued to stare at her. Flora had been placed at the center of them as they chatted and he smiled slightly. He found himself glad that she had found protectors when he knew how desperately his cousins hated her. She could not have had an easy time when she had to see them regularly.

"I don't know how anyone couldn't be interested in her," he mused softly. "It seems she is impossible not become friends with. And now I will go speak to her. Excuse me."

The two men murmured their acceptance of his leaving. He heard the continued interest and perhaps light strain in their voices at this turn of events, but he ignored it. He was going to Flora now. His focus was her, and he knew in his heart that focus was having less and less to do with the wretched duty his cousins had thrust upon his shoulders, or even the positive outcomes it could bring to his mother. No, this had everything to do with the lady herself. No matter how dangerous that fact was.

~

Roarke was coming toward her, and Flora's heart wouldn't stop pounding. It was the oddest reaction and one she couldn't remember ever having when it came to Stuart. She'd always been pleased to see him, of course. Welcomed being protected and loved by him, and returning the same. But this was… something else. Something primal that felt like it came from the deepest part of herself.

Something she needed to get under control. She forced a smile as he neared Flora and her friends. The other two duchesses did the same, though she recognized the hesitation in their expressions. Neither were certain about him yet and they would be protective until they were.

Which was good, since she was not thinking clearly.

"Your Grace," he said, looking at Flora.

All three ladies responded, "Yes?" And then all four of them laughed together.

He had a nice laugh. It made crinkles appear around those wonderful green eyes that now danced with humor. "Ah, I can see now why you all forgo the formalities when you are together," he said. "In this case, I was addressing our hostess. Flora."

It was the first time he'd said her given name out loud, at least to her. She couldn't help but suck in a breath even as she fought not to let anyone else in the room, least of all him, see how much the two syllables meant to her.

"Come, Valaria," Bernadette said. "I think the dukes are feeling abandoned."

Valaria shot Flora a quick look but didn't fight being all but dragged away. Flora smiled a little. At least she knew she had champions in this room.

"Mr. Desmond, I'm so glad you could come," she said, managing to turn to the polite interactions of a hostess to calm herself.

He arched a brow. "Now, now, are you going to address me formally while you expect me to do something different? That seems hardly fair."

She caught another breath. She hadn't thought about this part when she invited him to address them all informally. She would call him by his first name, which felt incredibly intimate. Why didn't it feel so intimate when she did so with Callum or Theo?

Probably because there wasn't some part of her which wanted to whisper their names in the dark, that hadn't woken up thinking about them, sheets tangled around her legs.

She blinked and forced those thoughts away. "I apologize. Roarke."

There, she had said it and his pupils dilated a fraction, like he liked hearing it. "You know," he said. "If we were at a ball, I would ask you to make room on your dance card for me. Perhaps I should ask now for the next time we share a ballroom, just in case yours fills up."

She wrinkled her brow as she stared up at him. He seemed earnest, not like he was teasing. "I, er, my dance card is never full."

The way he drew back and his eyes widened, it seemed that statement shocked him. "And why is that?"

"I have not danced since my husband died," she said softly.

He moved a little closer. It was all entirely acceptable. From across the room no one would think that something had shifted or that they were being inappropriate, but she knew. The air between them somehow felt thicker, hotter, and his gaze focused and steady on hers. "Not even once?"

Were they still talking about dancing or something else? She supposed it didn't matter, as the answer was the same. "Not even once."

The corners of his mouth lifted ever so slightly as if he were... relieved? Why, she couldn't say. It shouldn't matter to him who she danced with...or slept with, if that was what they were now talking about. He didn't know her. He certainly couldn't...want her. Not really. Wasn't this all her lonely imagination gone wild? Some fantasy she'd created after watching Valaria blossom under the attentions of Callum, or all the possibilities that always hung between Bernadette and Theo?

She stepped back. "If you'd like to dance with me at a future event, I suppose you'll have to come find me. And now I see my butler coming in to announce supper." She raised her voice for the room to hear. "Will you all join me in the dining room?"

Roarke hesitated a moment. As duchess she ought to have been escorted by the highest ranking in the room and she knew it. She knew if she turned to Callum or Theo that either would offer his assistance, as was proper. But she didn't want Callum or Theo, so she cleared her throat.

"Will you take me, Mr. Desmond?" she asked, her voice cracking slightly.

"Of course, Your Grace," he said, and held out his arm for her. She took it, feeling her fingers close against firm, warm muscle. Once again her body betrayed her, and with great effort she somehow managed not to sigh. She was becoming too obvious.

She just had to get herself together and remember her place. A place that very likely had almost nothing to do with this man.

~

Roarke had felt the pulsing attraction between he and Flora in the parlor before supper. He was no monk, he could tell when a lady wanted him. He could hear it in their breath and see it in their posture and expression. She had exhibited all of that and it had called to him in a way he knew was only trouble.

So the fact that she had avoided him ever since should have pleased him. At supper she had been polite, of course, the consummate hostess, but she hadn't lingered on him or asked too many questions. Afterward, she had asked Theo to escort her to the parlor for games and port as a group. She was never alone in conversation with Roarke.

But there was no relief, only regret that followed that set of facts. He *liked* talking to Flora. The years since his father's death, since his own foolish mistakes, had been painful. Lonely. Desperate. But being in the same room with this woman made that seem...distant for a little while.

He liked watching her light up, liked feeling her warmth like she was a candle in the night. He found himself wanting to chat with her more, about the world and people, about books and plays. To know her better, outside of the cruel errand his cousins had sent him on.

God, his errand. Hadn't he gathered enough information? He didn't believe Flora had ever taken a lover, not during or since her marriage. She had no engagement on the horizon, awaiting the moment she snatched away the money due to her on the three-year anniversary of her late husband's death. He would have bet his life on that fact.

Which meant his time with her would come to an end. He would make his report, his cousins would object and then steel themselves to paying her the extra funds their father's will required. They would pay him and give him a little more of a buffer for his mother's comfort.

This would be over.

He should let it be over.

Slowly he pushed off the fireplace where he had been standing since the group had finished a rousing game of charades, and moved toward Flora. She was also standing alone just then and she swallowed hard at his approach.

"It has been a lovely night," he said softly. "But I think it is time for me to go."

She blinked several times but then nodded. "I understand." She gave him what looked to be a forced smile and said to the group, "Mr. Desmond is the first to surrender. I shall walk him to the foyer."

He said his goodbyes to the rest of the group, finding them all friendly, even the hesitant ladies. It would be fun to be part of their circle like he had been tonight. Something else that could not be.

When he had finished, Flora motioned him toward the door. While a servant called for his horse, they stood together on the top step of her landing, cool autumn breeze stirring her hair and sending that warm scent of rosebuds to his nose again. God, but he wished he could surround himself in that, feel it permeate his skin and his mind and his soul.

A ridiculous notion.

"It was so nice of you to come tonight," she said, shifting slightly, worrying her hands like she was nervous.

He cleared his throat and then a question he had never intended to ask her tumbled from his lips. "Do you know the portrait painter, Ezra Pembroke?"

She blinked. "I...yes. I've seen several of his works...well, his public works."

He barely held back a little groan. So she knew about the celebrated artists private works, which were known to be erotic. That made his cock throb for a moment. "Er, well there is an exhibit of his *public* work at the Royal Museum. It just started. Would you like to...to accompany me to it on Monday afternoon?"

Her eyes went wide and she gaped for a moment, as if she were trying to process the question. As if she might not understand. "I...I..."

He held his breath. It would be better for them both if she said no. But God did he want her to say yes. To have that tour of a beautiful place be the end to this strange connection between them rather than a night at her home where he had secretly gathered information about her.

"I would enjoy that, Mr. Desmond. Roarke."

His knees nearly buckled under him and he smiled as his horse was brought to the drive. "Wonderful. Please let me know if you have any other engagements on Monday and I'll send information over about the exhibit to best fit your schedule."

She nodded and they stood there for an awkward moment. He should swing up on his horse and ride away. But he didn't want to. What he wanted to do was step in closer, touch her face, drop his mouth to hers and learn if she tasted as good as she smelled.

Her gaze fluttered away from his, as if she had read his thoughts. Her cheeks brightened with color in the dim light from the house behind them.

"Good night," he managed to croak out, and then did what he had to do. He rode away from her.

And was glad it wasn't for the last time after all.

CHAPTER 6

Flora knew she shouldn't be so excited about an afternoon at the museum. After all, she'd been there many times, enjoyed many exhibits with her husband and friends. And wasn't that all Roarke Desmond was? A friend. A new friend. But a friend, nonetheless. Anything else that her body felt when she was close to him was merely a biological response. She could ignore that.

But no matter how many times she repeated that to herself, let the word *friend* hang in her brain...always with a question mark after it...it didn't ring true. So she had changed her gown five times, fixed and refixed her hair, fiddled with jewelry and pinched her cheeks and checked the clock until all she could hear was its loud, echoing, accusatory tick in her head.

What was she doing?

Yes, of course, her lady's maid, Joy, would be with her. There was nothing untoward about going to a public exhibit with a gentleman. Of course people would whisper, but they whispered anyway. In the end, this excursion was harmless.

And yet it didn't feel harmless. It felt thrilling and exciting and a little like a betrayal of the marriage vows she'd taken so long ago. Ones that certainly didn't carry forward into her widowhood. But she could call Roarke her friend all day long and make excuses, but she knew she didn't want him for a friend. She wanted to spend time with him and have him spear her with that incredibly intense stare that seemed to curl her toes in her slippers.

She heard a knock at the front door and staggered to a stop in her pacing of the front parlor. He was here. He was early. Did that mean he was as eager as she was to spend time together? And if so, what did that mean? Did she have to do something? Her marriage had been arranged, papers signed by men of power with little thought to her wants or needs.

If something did happen with Roarke Desmond, that would be at her own choice and pleasure. So how did one proceed with such a thing?

"Your Grace?"

She clasped her hands together and looked at Hendricks with as much serenity as she could muster under the circumstances of her racing mind and heart. "Yes?"

"The Duchess of Tunbridge is here to see you," he said.

It was as if someone had deflated Flora. She felt her face fall and hated herself for it. Of course she was pleased to see Bernadette. She likely needed to see a friend, an *actual* friend with no question mark after that label, in order to get her mind right.

"Of course. Send her to me."

Hendricks inclined his head, and within less than a minute Bernadette entered the room, a bright smile on her face. One that fell the instant she saw Flora. "Oh goodness, what is *that* expression?" she asked.

Flora shook her head. "Nothing at all. I'm sorry to be a rude hostess, but I am going to be leaving soon. Mr. Desmond and I are to go to—"

Bernadette caught her breath. "Oh, heavens! The Pembroke exhibit. How could I have forgotten? I'm so sorry!"

"Nothing to be sorry about," Flora said. She caught her breath to say more. To confess her tangled feelings to Bernadette, but they wouldn't seem to come out. She didn't know how to say what she felt. What she was experiencing. And she didn't want to be seen differently for those feelings if she did find the words to speak them.

So instead she caught her breath. "You—you should come with us!" she burst out, and immediately hated herself for the suggestion. It made it all too clear that she didn't *want* to share her time with Roarke. Which in turn made it more obvious she needed to do just that.

"Come with you?" Bernadette repeated blankly. "Why in the world would you suggest such a thing? Are you merely trying to put up walls between you and this man?"

Of course that was exactly why, but Flora folded her arms. "What a ridiculous notion. Mr. Desmond and I barely know each other. He means nothing to me."

Bernadette pursed her lips. "I know you and Valaria think I'm a bit innocent. And perhaps I am. But I'm not a fool, you know. I can see that you did your hair just so. It looks lovely, by the way."

Flora touched her hair without thinking and then frowned. "I only wanted to look nice for the exhibit."

"And you're wearing the gown that best shows off your figure. And your eyes are fearful, but if I say *Roarke*...there, they dance just the tiniest bit." She moved forward and caught Flora's hands. "It is *fine* for this to mean something, Flora. You've been a widow a long time and if you choose to move forward, that is your right. It's also fine to have attraction that means *nothing* deeper than that you wish to spend time in the company of a handsome man. *All* of it is fine and you shouldn't wind yourself up in such knots trying to make it unimportant."

Flora's breath hitched and she blinked at the sudden stinging behind her eyes. "I don't know what to do if it means something. If I want something."

Bernadette's gaze softened, but she didn't get to say anything else. There was another knock at the door, and this time they both knew it was Roarke, right on time now.

Hendricks brought him to the room, and Flora noted his surprise to see Bernadette, even though he said, "Ah, Your Graces. What a pleasure to find two such lovely ladies waiting for me."

Bernadette smiled. "You are too kind. I hear you are taking Flora to the Pembroke exhibit. It should be wonderful. All of London is abuzz about it."

There was a brief moment where Roarke's eyes moved to Flora and she saw a flaring heat there. But then it was gone. Perhaps she had imagined it. "Yes," he said slowly.

"Well, I shall leave you to it and head back home for my own afternoon." She linked arms with Flora and together they all walked to the foyer. They had decided to take her carriage because Roarke only had his horse. Joy appeared from seemingly nowhere and stood by the carriage door, ready to take her place as chaperone.

"Let me help you," Roarke said to her softly, stepping away from Bernadette and Flora to do just that.

When he was out of earshot, Bernadette leaned in closer. "Just have fun, Flora. Don't make it more complicated than that."

She nodded and let Bernadette release her. Her friend waved to them both and then started up the Row back to her home.

Roarke turned back to Flora and his gaze flitted over her. "You look lovely."

She shifted slightly and tried not to run her hands over herself reflexively. "Thank you."

He offered a hand and she stared at it. His fingers were encased on brown leather gloves, but she knew when she touched him that she'd feel the reaction anyway. She had the last time she'd taken his arm. A thrill and a terror all at once. Something that made her far too aware of her own body and the nearness of him.

"Thank you again," she croaked, and finally took his extended fingers, leaning slightly on him as she took her place beside Joy in the carriage. Roarke his across from Flora. She noted how his bigger body filled the seat, how his shiny boot rested just next to her slipper.

When was the last time she'd been so aware of another person? She couldn't recall it and that made her feel terrible. It should have been Stuart, shouldn't it? She should have been able to recall feeling this thrill for the man she'd married, loved, genuinely missed.

"Are you a fan of museums in general?" Roarke asked, and she shook away the darker thoughts. Gracious, she was not going to be much of a pleasant companion if she was so serious and dour and lost in tangled emotions.

"Er, yes," she stammered. "I'm a great fan of art and attend any exhibit I can. I'm also a member of Lady Lena's Salon, so I enjoy the readings and lectures there, as well."

Roarke's eyebrows lifted with interest and she blushed. She hadn't been trying to brag, but Lady Lena's was a sought-after membership and a lovely escape for those who belonged.

"I've heard a great deal about the salon," he said. "Is it as wonderful as everyone implies?"

"Even more wonderful," she said with a smile. "Over the summer they did a lecture series about new discoveries in the field of amphibians. We had a spirited discussion about the recent population reduction of native tree frogs here in England."

He tilted his head and she stopped talking. Did he find this boring? Stuart certainly had, though he'd indulged her. Was she being silly in being enthralled about such things? She knew not everyone was enraptured by knowledge.

But then Roarke leaned closer. "The species is under threat?"

He seemed genuinely engaged and her heart fluttered. "Potentially," she said. "And the researcher showed us drawings and talked about their habitats. I've never been so interested in frogs in my life."

He smiled then and she caught her breath. Goodness but he was handsome. Why did he have to be so handsome? "Magnificent," he said, and he could have been describing himself.

She thought of what Bernadette had said to her earlier in the day. That she was *allowed* to think him handsome, to like spending time with him, whether it led to anything or not. That she was free and shouldn't tie herself in knots about whatever thrill of attraction Roarke inspired.

She shifted. "You know, salon members are allowed to bring a guest to any lecture. I normally take Bernadette when the subject interests her, but she mostly comes to the author readings."

"Not a tree frog person?"

She laughed. "I think Bernadette would be snoring in three minutes if I tried to talk to her about tree frogs. Her eyes would glaze right over." Flora shook her head. "She's brilliant about music or books, but I don't even think she likes frogs."

"Capital offense," Roarke laughed.

"Yes. Clap her in leg irons!" She swallowed hard. "If-if you'd like to join me at the salon some time, I'd be happy to be your hostess."

There was a flicker of something that came over his expression. Something like longing, only it was gone so quickly she had to think she imagined it. His smile became more false as he nodded. "If we are both in Town at the same time, that would be a very kind offer."

Her brow wrinkled. Somehow she had expected a more enthusiastic response after his questioning and gentle teasing. Lord, but this was difficult. She'd never had to read a man before, judge his interest. It was unendingly frustrating.

The carriage made a wide turn and she pushed back the curtain. "We're arriving," she said, happy to change the subject.

Soon they would have art to discuss and hopefully she wouldn't make an awkward mess of herself while they did so. Hopefully.

Roarke had hoped that when he and Flora were walking the halls of the museum, staring at portraits together, that he would be less taken by her. After all, they would have more space between them than they'd shared in the carriage. But now they had been roaming the halls for twenty minutes, looking at the portraits collected for the Ezra Pembroke exhibit, and he found himself even more aware of her.

They felt more alone together, for one thing. The museum was not busy on this day and her lady's maid had stepped away, no longer right between them. Taking in art felt more intimate than he'd expected. He could hear Flora's intake of breath whenever she looked at a piece that moved her. See the intensity of her stare when she leaned closer to look at a particular brush stroke.

He cleared his throat. "What do you think of his work, Your Grace?"

She pivoted toward him. "It's everything I've heard and more," she gushed, her hands lifting to her heart. She looked just as enraptured as she had when she talked about nature in the carriage, and he was just as taken by her enthusiasm.

"Not only is he a talented artist who can capture the true look of a subject—some of them almost look alive, like I could have a conversation with the piece as easily as the person—but there is emotion there," she continued. "Sometimes that's missing in these types of work."

"I tend to agree. It's what sets Pembroke aside. Like this one." He pointed toward a portrait of the Duke and Duchess of Abernathe, a golden couple of the day. Together they moved to it.

Flora let out a sigh. "It really does look like her."

"You know her?" Roarke asked.

"Just a little," Flora said. "She's very kind, and that kindness is reflected in her expression here. But it's more than that, isn't it?"

He nodded, looking at the composition of the piece. The lady was seated, cat winding around her feet. Her husband stood slightly behind her, his hand on her shoulder. A pose like a dozen others, but for the details Pembroke had added.

"Look at how his fingers are slightly curled in the areas where they touch her skin," Roarke said softly. "And how he's turned a little toward her."

Flora's breath was short. "And she's looking up at him, isn't she? Her expression has a…a…"

"Heat," he said. "There is a heat to it. And one grounded in reality, if the stories of the great love match of the Abernathes are to be believed."

"It is." There was a wistfulness to her voice when she said it. "No one who met them could deny it. It's a wonderful portrait. So special, I'm glad they agreed to let it be displayed for this exhibit."

They stood together in front of the portrait for a moment longer and then Roarke cleared his throat. The room felt a little warm now. His clothes a bit too tight all of a sudden. He was about to move on to one of the singular subjects for a bit of a break from the intimacy of what he and Flora had discussed, but she said something that stopped him short.

"I wonder if the same comes through in his…his other work."

She said it so softly he might not have heard it if he were a foot further way. But he wasn't and every word hit him in the gut. A little lower than the gut.

"His other work," he repeated slowly. "Yes, you said something about his public pieces a few days ago, as well. What do you know about Pembroke's *other* work, Flora?"

She glanced up at him, blue eyes holding his, pupils dilated with…oh, he recognized that flare of desire. It called to his own wildly inappropriate draw to her. He didn't want to take advantage. And yet she made it very difficult not to…to touch her. To pull his glove off, finger by finger, and drag those same digits down her bare arm until she sighed. Until she melted.

What would she look like if she melted?

Her cheeks flared with color. "People whisper," she said, her voice low, shaky. "I'm a widow, you know. They don't feel such a drive to protect me from delicate subjects. Scandalous ones. I know that Pembroke does a very different kind of painting for special clients. Have you…have you ever seen that work?"

He swallowed hard. She was talking about Pembroke's erotic work. Most of it was never displayed, but created only for clients willing to pay handsomely for the privilege of posing at their most intimate. But a few of his pieces had been shown in exclusive clubs like the Donville Masquerade. They were shocking and powerful. Over time more and more people had wanted to look at the erotic mingling of bodies, most of their owners unidentifiable in the portraits Pembroke chose to put on display.

"You know…" he began, and then cut himself off with a shake of his head.

She stared at him. "What were you going to say?"

Oh, he was going too far. And it had nothing to do with the horrible bargain he'd made with his cousins, nothing to do with protecting his mother. No, what he was about to say…suggest, was only about her.

"There is a small collection of those pieces here, as well," he said.

Her eyes went wide and wild at the words. "What?"

"But they've only made admission available to the gentlemen."

She pursed her lips. "Are the paintings only *of* gentlemen?"

He shook his head. "No. Almost no single figures, if I understand correctly. Couples or…er…more."

"More!" Her voice lifted and she looked around to see if someone had heard. But they were alone in this particular gallery except for Joy, who was all the way across the room, working on needlepoint rather than enjoying the paintings. She seemed entirely engrossed in that, as well.

He nodded. "Pembroke's erotic work can be shocking." Her breath was very short now. Shaky. "Would you…would you like to see it?"

He shouldn't have asked her that. Shouldn't have suggested such a wicked thing to a lady at all, not that a lot of ladies hadn't enjoyed the displays when they were at the higher quality hells. But this was different. He doubted Flora had a membership to such a club as the Donville Masquerade. Doubted she'd let herself come undone and explore all the wicked and wild things she wanted or felt.

He wondered what they were and what it would look like if she let go.

Her hands were trembling at her sides and she nodded shakily. "I…would," she whispered. "But I can't, can I?"

"It's quiet," he said, taking her elbow and quickly guiding her from the room. Her maid didn't even look up as they slipped past. He took Flora down a hallway, past other paintings from other artists outside the special exhibit. They twisted and turned through the halls until they came to a little darker area, hidden from the main view.

"You know this so well?" she murmured.

He shrugged. "They do exhibits that are limited to men from time to time. I know where they put them so they aren't easily found." He looked down the hallway. "There is no guard. We could look in for a moment. But only if you want to. The pieces are likely quite shocking."

"I want to," she whispered, but he felt her trembling against his side. He kept a grip on her elbow, in case she had a poor reaction to what they would see.

He pulled the dark curtain back and they stepped into the tiny gallery. There were only four portraits on display here, but they were immediately gripping. It was the same two models, though their faces were obscured, painted in various erotically charged positions. And he had no idea how Flora would respond.

CHAPTER 7

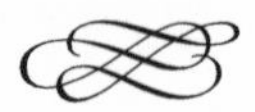

Flora didn't know where to look. She wanted to look at everything in that shocking room, drink in every image, but they overwhelmed her. The emotions she had seen in the more public photos were also here in these erotic ones, but multiplied by the nakedness of the couple's bodies, by the stark passion of their half-hidden expressions.

She was shaking as she moved to the piece closest to the door. In it the lady straddled the man, her bare thighs gripping his. Her head was dipped back and though her identity wasn't clear, her mouth was visible just at the top of the frame and twisted in a gasp of pleasure. His hands cupped her naked backside, fingers digging into soft flesh, a white-knuckled grip of pleasure.

She could almost feel that pressure herself, wondered what it would be like to be claimed with such fervor. "Oh," she murmured, without meaning to say anything.

"Too much?" Roarke asked. She jumped at the realization that he was standing just at her side, watching her look at such wicked things.

What could she say to him without revealing her arousal and

interest and desires that suddenly burned through her skin, in her blood, in a way she'd never allowed herself to feel?

So she said nothing, pretended she hadn't heard the question, and went to the second piece. This one appeared to be the same lady as in the first painting, the same gentleman lover. Pembroke's erotic muses, perhaps?

The faceless lady was turned toward the observer, the man at her back, his lips against her throat. A big hand covered one of her breasts. The other was bare, the dark nipple pebbled with desire. Her lover's second hand was between her legs, covering her as he pleasured her. But what was more shocking was that a second man's hand rested on the faceless lady's hip, paint slashed across his lean fingers. Like the artist had placed himself into the image with the other two.

Flora pivoted in surprise at such a thing, but when she stepped forward she collided into Roarke's chest and nearly tipped herself over. He caught both her elbows, tugging her closer to keep her from tumbling herself onto her arse.

She looked up at him, his expression stormy in the dimly lit gallery. He looked wild and untamed in that moment, like the very portraits before them. His hands were smooth on her skin, leather against flesh, for he hadn't removed his gloves yet. She wanted him to. Wanted to feel him against her in some echo of the erotic images before them.

He could have stepped away. She was steady now. Only he didn't. He continued to stare down at her, hands holding her firmly, her chest pressed to his chest. And oh, she wanted him to kiss her. She wanted him to back her into the darkest corner of the room and kiss her until she couldn't breathe or think or feel anything but him. *That* was what she wanted, so clear a desire that her head spun.

Only he didn't. As much as he looked like he wanted to do just that, as much as his breath stirred her lips because he was so close, he stepped away. "I-I think I hear someone in the hall."

She blinked. It would not do to be caught looking at such wicked things with a gentleman. To be found in his arms. She had a lot of freedom as a widow, yes. But that would cause talk no matter what.

"I think there is a back exit here," he said, and motioned to another curtain at the opposite side of the room. She followed him, noting that he no longer touched her, didn't take her arm. She tried not to look at the remaining two erotic portraits, each more passionate than the last, for fear she'd lose herself all over again.

They stepped into the hall, which now felt unbearably bright and cool. Almost dizzying because it was all so normal and what she felt was so foreign. Like she didn't belong in her own heated, aching body. Was this desire? She'd thought she knew it. Would have said she felt it during her marriage. But this was something far more intense, powerful, overwhelming.

"Your Grace!" Joy's voice dragged Flora from her spinning thoughts and she was just as happy for it, even as her cheeks heated when her maid rushed to her side. Would she know? Would she see? "My apologies, Your Grace, I didn't see you leave the other gallery."

Flora glanced back at Roarke. He was watching her, his green gaze focused on her, sending tingles up her back. She swallowed hard and tried to make her voice normal as she said, "No apologies. Mr. Desmond and I were just exploring some of the...some of the other rooms."

"Would you like to look at the main halls now?" Roarke asked, his voice so calm and so normal.

What she wanted to do was to flee into the street, run from these aching needs burning inside of her, run from the man who had almost kissed her but hadn't. Run from the feelings stirred inside her.

Only that would only make this all worse. So instead she inclined her head like she'd been trained to as a lady and said, "That sounds lovely. Lead the way, Mr. Desmond."

They walked through the other galleries together, ones Flora had seen and enjoyed many times. Only now there was no hesitating. No pressing close together to admire an image or discuss their thoughts on a composition. They marched through the spaces, only giving cursory looks to the artwork. They hardly spoke at all anymore. How she hated that. Hated that the near kiss had ruined what had been a lovely day that she'd enjoyed.

Hated that she still wished he'd kissed her there in the dimness, surrounded by those erotic pieces that Society would say a lady's eyes shouldn't see.

Soon enough they were coming to the end of their day, and Flora could see Roarke looking toward the huge doors that led back to the drive.

"Should I fetch your carriage, Your Grace?" Joy asked softly.

"I'll do it," Roarke said, and stepped away.

Flora's heart sank. He didn't even want to be alone with her in this big, public foyer. Was that because he didn't want to discuss what had happened? Did he fear she would be angry or upset? Or worse, that she wouldn't be? Oh, this was so complicated. She didn't know how to read a man's interest. She thought she'd felt it, but then he pushed it aside and she couldn't find it anymore.

She let out a long sigh without meaning to and Joy glanced at her. "Are you well, Your Grace?"

She looked at her lady's maid with what she hoped was a slight smile rather than a grimace. "Oh yes. Just difficult to leave the museum, as always. I hope you enjoyed yourself."

Joy gave a quick nod, though her gaze darted away. Flora's heart sank all the more. Stuart had never been all that interested in art. He'd taken her to museums as a kindness to her, and listened to her prattle on with an indulgent smile. Valaria couldn't go out still due to her mourning. And while Bernadette also came along with Flora when she asked, she was likely as interested as Joy. So Roarke had been the first person in ages she had attended a museum with and really felt his thrill as deeply as her own.

That had been real. She knew that if nothing else.

But here he came, striding across the foyer of the museum,

expression taut. He didn't look thrilled anymore. "It should be here momentarily," he said. "Shall we?"

He motioned to the door, almost like he couldn't wait to leave. She ignored the faint sting of disappointment in her eyes and moved toward the front doors. He allowed her footman to help her into her carriage as he discussed something with the driver. Didn't want to touch her now, it seemed. Joy followed and then he entered the carriage.

The drive back to Kent's Row was far quieter and even more awkward than the one over. She found herself staring out the window after a few moments, trying to lose herself in the scenery instead of him. It couldn't be him. And of course, why should it be? She had resigned herself long ago to the life of an independent widow. She couldn't let a flash of desire, a hint of attention, change that. It was all very silly.

They arrived at her home and she was helped down by a servant. Joy bobbed out a curtsey and entered the house to give Flora a moment alone with her guest before his horse was brought back.

"I—" Flora began, uncertain what to say.

"I'm sorry," he interrupted, his green gaze casting away from hers like he couldn't bear to look at her.

She blinked. "For…for what?"

"I ought not to have shown you the private display," he said softly. "You are a lady and it wasn't my place to stand beside you and be with you when you looked at such shocking things."

Her lips parted. "You think I was offended?"

He glanced back at her. "Weren't you?"

She should have said yes. She supposed she'd been trained all her life that her answer to a question like that should be yes. That looking at those deeply intimate and erotic pieces should have created a ricochet of outrage and embarrassment.

She moved a little closer to him and heard him take in the slightest of breaths. She liked that little intake—it felt like it meant he was moved by her.

"I wasn't offended," she said, wishing her voice could be stronger, but only able to make it just above a whisper. "I was shocked, yes. I think anyone would be to see such things, and in a public space. But I was...*moved*...by what I saw. So if the reason you turned away from me in that room or afterward was that you thought you had hurt or insulted me, I will assure you now that is the furthest thing from what I felt when I looked at Pembroke's private work with you."

He held her stare a beat, two, and this time she wasn't confused by what she saw in those green depths. He wanted her. She could practically feel the heat radiating from him, warming her down to her toes. To between her legs where everything felt a little achy and empty.

"I'm glad to hear it," he said, and then jolted as his horse was brought to them. He glanced back at her. "I should...I should go, Flora. Your Grace."

She bent her head. "I see."

"You don't. But I promise you that it is better for you. I shouldn't have stolen this little extra time with you this afternoon, pretended that I could have it. But I enjoyed every moment, Flora." He drew a little closer. "*Every* moment. Goodbye."

He swung up on his horse and swiftly urged the animal down her drive and back out onto the street. She watched him go, heart throbbing, and only when he had disappeared from view did she realize he had said goodbye to her. Not good afternoon, not good day...goodbye.

Like she would never see him again. And her heart ached that it was a possibility.

Roarke knew he had been difficult to read during his day at the museum with Flora. He also sensed that his hot-and-cold demeanor had confused and potentially hurt her, and he hated himself for that. When he'd asked her to see the exhibit, he had wanted it to be a last good time together, without any thought to his cousins and their wicked bargain with him to investigate Flora.

But it had turned into something far more. Why had he taken her into the private room? Why had he watched her become aroused by those wicked, beautiful, passionate images Pembroke had painted of his lovers? And why the hell had he almost kissed her?

Worse, the real question that bombarded him, tormented him, was why *hadn't* he kissed her? He should have kissed her in that gallery. He should have pressed her against the wall, felt her mold to him and moan against him. He should have given her what her sharp breaths and unfocused stare revealed she needed so badly.

He grunted as he adjusted himself, his cockstand desperately uncomfortable when he was riding a horse. He deserved that. He deserved worse, truth be told.

He turned up a lane and realized where he was guiding his horse without even meaning to. To his cousin's home, the ducal estate where he'd been given his orders and turned into a vile spy what let like a lifetime ago. And of course that was where he needed to go. To end this.

She deserved that.

He rode the remaining distance and pulled to a stop in front of the large, beautiful home. He looked up as he swung down and handed over his reins to the stablehand who raced to greet him.

He'd never had many thoughts about this place. It was just a big house where he'd visited his aunt a few times as a young boy. Then, after the death of his father, the decline of his mother's health and his own foolish fall, it had become a prison where he had no choice but to come to beg for money from his cousins.

But now he looked up and up and saw the place where *Flora* had lived. Flora had stood at these windows and looked down at arriving friends and family, probably smiled before she came down to greet them. Flora had arranged the parties and balls, Flora had walked with her late husband through the gardens. Flora had lost his uncle here, setting her on the path where she now stood. Where she now looked at Roarke with a trembling need that called to him so loudly and keenly.

One he couldn't respond to. She didn't know who he was, not really, she didn't know how he was related to her sad past. She didn't know that he had been sent as a infiltrator and a betrayer. He didn't want her to know.

So he'd end this now. Sharp and firm and in a way that would cut his cousins' machinations off at the knees. He only hoped they would all be here.

His cousin's butler met him at the door and frowned. "Were you expected, Mr. Desmond?"

Roarke pursed his lips. "No," he admitted. "But if you tell the duke that this is about the dowager, I'm sure he will wish to see me."

Both the butler's brows raised slightly and he inclined his head rather than simply dismissing Roarke as it was clear he'd been about to do. "I will ascertain if His Grace is in residence."

"And the others," Roarke said sharply. "If my other cousins are here, I want to see them, too."

The man looked irritated to be ordered around so by a man with no title, but didn't argue. He simply pointed Roarke to a parlor off the foyer and went down the hallway toward the back of the house. Roarke entered the room, rubbing suddenly sweaty palms against his trouser legs.

He knew what he had to do. But he also knew these actions might...probably would...have consequences. Potentially life-changing ones. But there was no going back now.

CHAPTER 8

In a few interminable moments, the door to the parlor opened and Roarke turned to watch his three cousins come in. They looked a bit windblown, and he realized they must have been out on the veranda or in the garden together.

"Good Lord, Roarke, you could have sent word," Thomas snapped as an abrupt greeting, even as he slammed the door behind the three of them. "We were in the middle of a garden party and there are important guests to get back to. What could you possibly want?"

Roarke arched a brow. "I thought you were *desperate* for news of the dowager."

He was careful not to call her Flora, even though her name was on the tip of his tongue. They would pounce on that like rabid dogs and he was in no mood to explain himself to them.

"Thomas, let him speak," Gertrude insisted, stepping forward. Her eyes shone with excitement, with cruel glee. "Tell us what you've learned, not that we haven't already guessed."

Philip's eyes were just as bright as his sister's though Roarke thought for a different reason. "She's been whoring around, hasn't she? She has lover, kept secret so that she may claim what is not rightfully hers. Tell us everything, spare *no* detail."

Roarke winced at the harshness of his tone, and because when Philip said *lover*, Roarke couldn't help but picture Flora staring up at him in the gallery, her breath short as he fought the wave of desire between them. Whatever man would one day be Flora's lover was truly lucky. Roarke tried not to hate him.

Thomas glared at his brother. "Christ, Philip, enough." He stifled a yawn. "Do go on with it, though, Roarke. I'd like to get back to drinks and fine ladies, not waste more time on our father's concubine."

Roarke clenched his hands at his sides. God, but they were like vultures, waiting for him to deposit a carcass to pick. But he would not feed them. Not even if it meant denying his own supper. He could starve a little. He could find some other way to protect his mother.

"I've investigated the dowager extensively," he said. "And despite what you three think of her, she is not doing anything untoward or secretive. There are no gentleman callers, let alone clandestine lovers who darken her hallways. She is just as she seems, an independent woman living her life as best she can."

For a moment the room was dead silent as his cousins digested his statement. The three of them stared at him, color leaving their wretched cheeks all at once. He almost smiled at their horrified expressions, as they fully grasped that they couldn't steal the inheritance her husband had rightfully set aside for Flora, after all.

"You're lying," Gertrude whispered at last, her lips trembling and her eyes filling with tears.

"She *must* be doing something," Thomas hastened to add, shaking his head as if he were thoroughly confused by the news.

Philip, though, began to pace the room, almost like an animal. "She's a manipulator and a thief and a...a *whore* who...who spins men around her finger—those truths will not change."

It took everything in Roarke not to snap at the assessment and the cruelty that went with it. He shook his head. "Just because *you* all would deceive in order to obtain an inheritance doesn't mean she would." Gertrude let out a gasp, but he didn't allow her or Philip to speak again. Instead, he glared at Thomas. The new duke was the one who mattered. The other two would just follow along with whatever he said. "Now I did what you asked, *Your Grace*. This is over. Leave her alone."

Thomas stepped closer, tilting his head to look closer at Roarke. "You are defending her rather strenuously, *cousin*. I wonder why that is."

Roarke had wanted to punch his cousin multiple times over the years. Mostly when they were children and Thomas had bullied him or those around them. But he never had. And he couldn't rise to the bait and do it now, either. It would only make things worse, even if the crunch of his fist against Thomas's cheek would be infinitely satisfying. But he had more than just himself to think about.

Through gritted teeth, Roarke said, "I found Her Grace to be charming and honest. And it's clear that she truly loved your father, which is what one would hope you would have wanted for him in his last few years. You waste your time plotting against her when you should just move on with your lives." He shook his head. "God's teeth, you three have everything you have ever wanted, don't you? The title, the money, the entail, the homes? *Move on*. And I shall do the same."

He turned but before he had taken one step Thomas's voice stopped him. "You want your money, don't you?"

He shut his eyes and groaned. The fucking money. He'd love to just storm out in a display of strength, but there was two-hundred-fifty pounds on the line. Once he'd fixed the window and the mantel in his mother's home and given Hilde a little extra for all her hard work, there was nothing left of the first half of his blood money. He couldn't afford to turn away.

He turned back, his stomach roiling with self-disgust. "You can deposit it in my account."

"And what if it could be more?" Thomas asked softly. "Say twenty times more."

Roarke stared, and Gertrude and Philip both pivoted to Thomas. Roarke struggled to do the math his cousin was suggesting in his head. Simple math made impossible by shock.

"You want to give him five *thousand*?" Philip shrieked, filling in the number Roarke couldn't find. His face was turning red and his fists shook at his sides in what seemed to be pure rage at the idea. Gertrude had been standing next to him, but she took several steps away at the reaction as Philip continued, "What could *possibly* be worth that? Whatever it is, I'll take care of it myself and you can give me the blunt."

Thomas waved his hand at his brother, silencing him with a glare. "This is between our cousin and me. Sit down and shut up."

He did so, or at least Roarke assumed he did. He couldn't see Philip or Gertrude anymore because he couldn't tear his dizzy gaze away from Thomas. His voice cracked as he asked, "What the hell are you talking about?"

"I know you despise coming to me, being beholden to me," Thomas said. "You may think me a fool, or yourself a good actor, but I see your disgust, your disdain written all over your face, Roarke. Even as you try to be polite while you beg me to support you. To support your darling, desperate *mother*."

Roarke turned his face, bile rising in his throat. His cousins never asked about his mother. She wasn't related to them by blood, so they didn't care about her. It was for the best, really. He didn't want them to be interested in her.

And now Thomas was. But Roarke said nothing because there was nothing to say. He wouldn't deny the truth, he had lied enough in the last week.

"Five thousand pounds is a tidy sum," his cousin continued with a smirk. "Half of what that bitch would inherit if she *is* truly maintaining a pure widowhood."

Roarke winced at the word *pure*, as if Flora's desire were filthy to be ashamed of. The woman had loved and supported her husband, she had remained alone for nearly three years after he was gone. Had she not earned pleasure and fun and love? It wasn't wrong or dirty for her to desire those things.

"You could get your mother out of the hovel she currently lives in," Thomas said. "Have more care for her in her declining years. That matters to you, doesn't it?"

Roarke nodded slowly. "Yes," he choked out.

"And when it's all done and she's comfortable," Thomas went on, almost seductively. "You could even get yourself out of the mud. Perhaps even invest again and see if it would turn out better for you this time."

Roarke thought of Grayson Danford and his offer to let him invest in his steam engine. He believed in the project, believed in the payout that could come from it down the line. And yes, five thousand pounds would allow him to both take part in that possibility and create a real future for himself. And more importantly, for the last years of his mother's life.

But at what cost?

"And why would you give me that?" he croaked. "You are so protective of the funds, I can't imagine you'd just give me half."

"I don't want *her* to have the money," Thomas continued, his eyes flashing with intense, almost frightening animosity briefly. "She's gotten enough. I'd be willing to part with half in order to make sure she never gets another hay penny."

Roarke looked at the door. He needed to leave. He had to walk away. Nothing was worth this.

"At least hear me out," Thomas insisted. "You might not hate what I will suggest so very much."

"What would you have me do?" Roarke whispered.

Thomas smiled. "Seduce her."

Roarke took a long step away as those two words hit him in the chest with the same power as a shotgun blast might have. "What?"

"Become her lover, thus helping her along so she will violate the terms of the second payout of the inheritance," Thomas said. "It seems as though that wouldn't be much of a chore if the way you look when you speak of her means anything."

Roarke shook his head. The world was spinning. The idea of seducing Flora sent a dozen images through his mind, none of them unpleasant. But when he looked at the smug expression on his cousin's face, that melted away. All he could see was rage. He stepped forward and grabbed for Thomas's lapels. He yanked his cousin closer and shook him.

"Fuck you," he hissed in Thomas's face.

Gertrude gasped from the settee behind them and Philip lunged forward as if he would attack, but Thomas raised a hand to stop him, then he jerked free, smoothing his jacket. "Or you could get nothing further from us," he snapped. "And starve like the pauper you'll be."

The world tilted. That suggestion would have consequences for more than just himself. But then again, he was tired, so tired, of groveling to these cruel animals who called themselves his family.

Perhaps this was the perfect time to walk away. To get out from under their thumbs, even if it meant more suffering for himself in the short term.

"I'll get an occupation," Roarke muttered, more to himself than to them. "I'll find something I can do and pay my own way."

He had no idea what that would be. He'd been raised with every advantage except competency. Men like him were told to shun employment, so he didn't even know the first step. But he could make it. He didn't know Theo or Callum well enough to beg them, but he could discreetly ask them to suggest him for a position. Perhaps even Grayson Danford would be open to using his talents, however small they might be.

"You'll get *nothing* if I spoil the waters wherever you go," Thomas promised with a slight smile. "Instead of giving that money to you, I'll track your every movement with the resources that five thousand can pay for. I will create any rumor I can to ruin your prospects if you do not bend to me. Before I'm finished, I'll make sure you can't work at the docks gutting fish."

Roarke stared at him, trying to find the boy he'd once known in the hard, spoiled man before him. "You hate me that much?"

"I hate *her* that much. With every fiber of my being, I hate her," Thomas said.

"Why?" Roarke breathed.

Thomas blinked, and there was a brief flash of pain over his face. Then it was gone. "She might have tricked my father into thinking she was worthy of our money and position, but I know better. She *never* should have been allowed into our home, shared our name, replaced our mother. Never. You have a choice. I can use you to simply ensure she gets nothing further. It will hardly hurt her, will it? She has the original fifteen-thousand, I couldn't take that if I tried. She won't suffer for what she never had. Or, you can thwart me, lose everything—your mother can lose everything. And then I will choose to punish Flora, instead. Truly punish her."

Roarke swallowed. "How?"

Thomas tilted his head and gave an ugly smile devoid of all warmth, laced with vicious intent. "If you won't, Roarke, then I'll hire someone *else* to seduce her. By *whatever* means necessary. So you will sit in your squalor alone, knowing your failed your family and wondering how exactly my minions will accomplish what I want."

"Thomas!" Gertrude gasped, stepped forward.

He glared at her. "Stay out of it."

Roarke swallowed back the bile that rose in this throat. He pictured some piece of shit going after Flora. Bothering her, tricking her, even hurting her in order to fulfill Thomas's demands.

He was left at a crossroads. If he agreed to this, he was the worst kind of bastard. He would use her desire for him against her and take what was rightfully hers as the payment.

But if he refused his cousin, he endangered his mother *and* Flora. He would fail them both rather than protect either one of them.

"You best answer faster, cousin," Philip said with a half-chuckle. "I can tell when my brother is serious and I already have some ideas in mind if you refuse."

Roarke glared at him. "I know he's serious."

Thomas's face was flat and emotionless. Like he felt nothing about this cruel suggestion. It was the same to him as demanding a servant do a better job at making a bed. The lives at stake, the destruction he would create…none of it mattered as long as he got what he wanted.

Roarke's mind spun. If he accepted Thomas's terms, at least he'd have time. Options.

"I want a thousand pounds up front," he croaked.

Thomas threw back his head and laughed. "Bold. But no. You can have another two-hundred fifty up front. And five hundred with your first progress report to me. The rest you won't see until you give me proof you've bedded her."

"Proof," he whispered. "What kind of proof do you think I can generate?"

"You'll think of something," Thomas said with a detached smile. "So what is your answer? I'm running out of patience."

With a small amount of money in his pocket up front, Roarke had breathing room. He could draw everything out, decide how to tell Flora the truth if it came to it.

At least that was how he justified it in his head.

"Fine," he whispered.

Philip pulled a face, as if he'd wanted to solve what the three of them considered a problem on his own. But he said, "I knew you weren't a fool."

Roarke *was* a fool for putting himself in this situation. But he said nothing.

"Excellent," Thomas said. "Now why don't you join us for the party. We can celebrate this partnership."

"Celebrate?" Roarke repeated. "There's *nothing* to celebrate. I'm leaving."

He turned on his heel, hearing his cousins' laughter behind him as he strode from the room, from the house and rode away. For now he had done enough to protect his mother. To protect Flora from his cousins.

But he had no idea how he would proceed. Because while the idea of seducing her, being close to her, was bewitching, the lies behind it shattered him. And yet he had no choice. Not anymore.

CHAPTER 9

Two days had passed since Flora's day at the museum with Roarke, since the near kiss that had never left her mind for one moment in the intervening time. She hadn't spoken to anyone about it. Bernadette and Valaria had asked questions about her museum day, probably suspected something when she was evasive in her answers, but she couldn't bring herself to say anything out loud about it. To admit everything that happened with Roarke, more to admit what she'd *wanted* to happen and dreamed about happening, was speaking out loud something wicked into the world. She wouldn't be able to take it back then. To explain it away.

So she kept it secret. And dreamed of Roarke even as she tried to accept that she might not see him again. He hadn't reached out after he left her on her drive. Hadn't come to call or bumped into her at the park, where she shamelessly looked for him. Even now she stood at her parlor window, looking out across the lane into the green expanse and…not seeing him lurking there.

"You are being ridiculous," she muttered to herself as she turned from the window and marched across the room to the sideboard to make herself a cup of tea. She had mooned enough over the man. It was time to regather herself and go back to her regular life.

But just as she lifted the teapot, she heard Hendricks clear his throat from behind her. She turned. "Yes?"

"A letter was just delivered, Your Grace." He held out the envelope on a silver platter and she took it.

"Thank you," she said with a smile as he exited the room.

It was probably from Bernadette or Valaria, inviting her to some gathering with Callum and Theo. Where she would be the odd one out. The only one without a gentleman to take her arm or look at her meaningfully. That had hardly ever bothered her before, but now...well, now it made her ache just a little.

She turned the envelope over and frowned. Her name was not written in either woman's hand. Her breath caught, hateful hope filling her chest as she broke the plain seal and unfolded the pages.

Your Grace,

May I call on you soon? I have something of importance to discuss.

Sincerely,

Roarke Desmond

She read and re-read the message several times, analyzing the swoops of the letters, the confidence of his hand. It hit her then, the fact she'd been trying to pretend away, suppress: she *liked* him. She wanted him. She didn't want to never see him again, she didn't want to pretend that he hadn't nearly kissed her. Perhaps she couldn't have put into exact words what she wanted him to do now, nor what she wanted, herself. But she needed to see him.

She scribbled a note asking him to call the next afternoon and handed it over to Hendricks before she wrapped herself in a shawl and made the short walk down Kent's Row to Valaria's home. When she was allowed in, she could hear her friend in the parlor, laughing with Bernadette. Good, they were both here. She needed them both, even if she might die of humiliation.

Valaria's butler led her to them and the ladies smiled as she entered the room.

"Oh, excellent!" Valaria exclaimed as she got up from the settee and crossed to kiss Flora's cheek. "You've decided to stop hiding in your house."

"Was it that noticeable?" Flora said with a shake of her head since she couldn't deny the truth.

Bernadette patted the seat Valaria had vacated, and Flora took it while Valaria moved to pour her tea. "It was," Bernadette said, rather apologetically. "Your excuses as to why you couldn't join us over the past few days have been rather forced."

Valaria gave her the tea. "Do you want to tell us what happened? Or would it be best to ignore it?"

Flora sipped her tea and girded up all her strength. "I'd love to ignore it. But that doesn't seem possible now. I…I need your help. So here I am."

Valaria took a place in a chair across from the settee, her brow furrowed. "That sounds dire. Are you well?"

"I'm not even sure," Flora whispered. "I can't even tell anymore."

"Start from the beginning," Bernadette urged gently. "And know we're here for you."

Flora sighed, set her teacup down and slowly told her two friends about what had happened at the museum. She told them about the erotic art, cheeks flaming as their eyes widened. And she told them about the near kiss, sparing no detail despite her discomfort in being so open with what had happened. Or almost happened.

"Oh," Valaria said when she had finished. "And he hasn't spoken to you since?"

"No," Flora said. "Until…until this afternoon when I received a message from him. He wants to see me and I sent word back for him to join me tomorrow afternoon."

Bernadette shook her head. "I can see why you've wanted to be alone. How confusing. Do you wish one of us to join you when he calls? Or perhaps both of us?"

"We'll happily be your guards and stare him down," Valaria added, her eyes flashing with protectiveness that Flora adored.

"No," she said slowly. "I-I don't need you to be there, as much as I appreciate the offer. I don't think I need a guard at all. What I need is…that is what I was hoping to talk to you about was…was…"

"Go ahead," Bernadette encouraged, taking both her hands and squeezing gently. "Anything."

"I wanted to ask you how one might go about seducing a man."

There, she had said it, and now she felt a little dizzy and hot. Worse, her two friends were staring at her like she'd just sprouted a second head or started speaking in tongues.

"I-I'm going to need you to clarify that," Valaria said, both eyebrows lifted in question. Bernadette said nothing, just blinked at Flora, expression lined in shock.

"I tried to not feel it," Flora began with a shake of her head. "I tried to talk myself out of it. But I *wanted* Roarke to kiss me at the museum. I was so disappointed when he didn't. Truth be told, I wanted him to do…to do more than kiss me." She lifted her hands to her face. "God, my cheeks are hot. I can't even speak about it."

"You're doing fine," Bernadette assured her, even though her voice was a little strained.

"I dream about him," she whispered, because she might as well complete the humiliation. "And he's doing a lot more than kissing me."

There was a heavy silence in the room and Bernadette nodded. "You are allowed to want a man." There was something wistful in her tone and Flora might have pushed the topic any other day, but today *she* needed help.

"Am I?" she asked. "I know neither of you had this experience and for that I'm sorry, but I did truly love Stuart. In the three years since his death, I've never even considered an affair or taken an interest in another person. I believed that I would likely live out the rest of my days as a widow, finding my satisfaction in my hobbies and my friends. I was content with that, or I thought I was. And then this man comes along and it's like a lightning bolt."

Valaria smiled slightly. "I know *that* feeling."

"I want to know what it would be like if he kissed me. I look at him and my insides do things they never did with Stuart. Is that a betrayal? It both feels like one and it also feels natural."

"Because it is!" Valaria burst out, passion lighting in her eyes. "We want as men want, we need as they do. I learned that with Callum. He made it safe for me to feel it. And you deserve passion and pleasure, Flora! You deserve to feel all those things and more. *If* this man wants you just as much. *If* he would protect you as you deserve."

"I think he would," Flora said. "I know he wanted me that day. I saw it in his eyes. All his hesitation, I think it is out of propriety. Or some belief that he shouldn't approach me for more due to my position in life. But if I made the first move, if I were brave enough to ask for what I want…he would be careful. He would be…"

"Passionate," Bernadette finished on a whisper. Almost a whimper. Both Valaria and Flora looked at her.

"Bernadette," Valaria said gently.

She shook her head. "Don't talk to me about it," she insisted. "I can't talk about it. Let's concentrate on Flora."

Flora was hesitant, but she could see that whatever Bernadette wanted, she truly wouldn't speak of it yet. And so she allowed herself to refocus on what she'd come to discuss.

"But I'm still at a loss at what to do," she said. "My marriage to Stuart was arranged, the fact that we would go to bed ordained by the vows we took. I didn't have to catch his attention in that way—I expected he would have me and he was always very gentle when he did. It was nothing like those paintings, at any rate. So I have no idea how to seduce someone."

Valaria let out a soft laugh. "You know, six months ago I would have told you I was the last person you should ask about seduction of a man."

"I'm still the last person you should ask," Bernadette said on a laughing sigh.

Valaria grinned at her. "We would have been three women at a loss. But I suppose time changes us all. So where do you want to start? I'll share whatever knowledge I have now."

"Please! Just start somewhere," Flora said, leaning forward. She noticed Bernadette was doing the same, as if they were both about learn at the knee of a master.

Valaria drew a deep breath. "I suppose let us start on the subject of kissing."

~

Roarke had felt sick when he left his cousin's home three days before. So many times he'd considered going back and telling him to sod off. But a visit to his mother had brought that up short.

She looked so small sometimes. And all she had was him and Hilde, who needed to be fairly compensated for her work. So he had no choice.

He'd also felt sick when he sent his message to Flora and received her invitation in return. He felt sick now as he rode up her drive to meet with her. What he wanted to do was tell her the truth. All of the truth.

Perhaps he still should and then they could work out together what to do next. Even though she would hate him.

He pulled up on her drive and swung down from his horse, patting the beast's shoulder absently before he handed over the reins to one of Flora's servants. The door to her home was already open, her butler awaiting him with a sharp expression on his face. Protective? Perhaps that was it. If true, it wasn't a surprise. A woman like Flora, who was so kind, likely inspired protective instincts from most decent people who met her.

Roarke didn't feel like a particularly decent person at present.

"Good afternoon, Hendricks," he said, handing over his gloves and hat.

"The duchess is expecting you," Hendricks said, leading him to the parlor off the foyer. "Please wait here for Her Grace."

He left then, off to find her, and Roarke paced the small room, running a hand through his hair absently, the terrible position he found himself in ricocheting through his mind.

His mother, with no protection because of him. Flora, hurt by what he had been told to do. And also thoughts of that day in the museum when she'd stared up at him and he'd wanted her so much. That hadn't been a game or a lie.

"Mr. Desmond." Her voice came behind him, and he turned to watch her enter the room.

His breath caught because she was even more beautiful than the last time he'd seen her. Her auburn hair was curled and plaited in an elaborate style, her blue eyes were bright and she wore a yellow gown with faint striping through the fabric. A silky sash settled just below her lovely breasts, accentuating her curvy figure and making him want to trace his hands along the lines of her.

No, he was definitely not decent.

"Your Grace," he said, stepping toward her.

She wavered before she glanced back at the door. Slowly she reached back, and then she did something unthinkable: she shut it.

He stared at her hand, still resting on the barrier, her eyes holding on him.

"I'm glad you sent your message, Roarke. I also wished to see you and wasn't brave enough to be the one to ask." She moved forward just a half-step and clenched her hands before her. "I haven't stopped thinking about you since I saw you last."

Her cheeks filled with pink color at that admission and her gaze darted away for a fraction of a moment before she seemed to force herself to look back. To hold his stare with a shaky boldness that made it feel like she was closer than she actually was.

He swallowed hard. "I'm sorry with how we left things," he said, hearing how rough his voice was with desire.

Her eyes widened and her mouth twitched like she wanted to smile. Like she was happy to hear him say such a thing. A wash of emotions hit him all at once. He felt want and need, and also self-loathing. In his mind, he could hear her sharp intake of breath when she'd looked at the erotic paintings, but it mixed with the cruel laughter of his cousins as they crowed about him accepting their wicked bargain. It collided with the tenor of his own lies, ones this woman didn't deserve.

"Flora, I must tell you something," he whispered.

She moved forward swiftly, her hands outstretched. "Please," she whispered. "Let me go first."

He bent his head. "Of course."

"I...I was married to a man much older than I was," she said softly, her cheeks blooming with even deeper color. Roarke forced himself to look at her then, to take in any information that would make him feel better about this situation.

"My parents insisted on the match, and why wouldn't they? Stuart was a duke, he was very well off. My dowry actually went straight into an account that was for me and is the money I inherited when he passed. He never used it for his own desires."

Roarke felt the color drain from his cheeks. So the fifteen thousand his cousins griped about hadn't even come out of their estate to begin with. The situation got worse and worse.

"But though I cared for him, truly loved him...I-I never felt the kind of stirring of what I felt standing next to you at the gallery. I never felt the passion I saw reflected in Pembroke's paintings." She shook her head. "Oh, I don't know how to do this."

He hesitated. "Do what?"

"Did you want to kiss me that day?" she whispered.

He stared at her. The fact that it wasn't perfectly clear to her was shocking to him. He hadn't hidden it well.

"Yes," he said. "There was no ulterior motive that day, Flora. No hidden reason. I stood next to you, watched how you reacted to the paintings and all I wanted to do when you looked at me, when you tumbled into my arms, was to kiss you. I didn't care about anything else. I didn't care about where we were. I wanted to kiss you more than I wanted to take my next breath."

He needed her to know that, even if she wouldn't fully understand that confession. Even if she didn't know what he meant by ulterior motives.

Her lips parted. "I don't think anyone has ever wanted me like that. I liked seeing it. I'm glad it was real." She shifted. "And I want… I want…"

She trailed off, struggling to find the words, and Roarke stepped forward, closing the distance between them. The stakes were so high now. He knew his mother might suffer if he didn't do what he'd been told to do. But he couldn't look at this woman and betray her trust. He *couldn't* play her for a fool.

"Flora, I really must tell you something," he said, his voice breaking, rough.

Her eyes went wide and she shook her head. "Oh please, don't tell me no."

"No?" he repeated softly, understanding and not understanding. Not believing. "No to what?"

She bit her lip and he followed the seductive scrape of her teeth against it. She reached out, resting her palms against his chest. They were as close as they had been in the gallery, only this time the door was closed. He doubted anyone would dare interrupt them here.

She stared up at him, blue eyes shimmering with unchecked, undeniable need. Everything else fell away in that moment, all his doubts, all his reasons, all his problems. There was only her. It was a respite. An oasis. He had never felt anything like it in his life and he found it impossible to turn away from it.

He felt her tremble as she pushed up onto her tiptoes and leaned in even closer. Their bodies touched from shoulder to knee, her warmth filled him, changed him. He was further changed when her mouth found his and she kissed him.

CHAPTER 10

Flora had always liked kissing. It felt so warm, so close, so intimate. But now she wasn't certain she was doing it right. After all, Roarke stood stock still, his mouth not moving beneath hers.

Until it did.

He made a low rumble in his chest that she felt ricochet through her entire body and then his arms closed around her, drawing her even tighter to him. He parted his lips, gently tracing the crease of her mouth with his tongue and she gasped against him, allowing him entry.

He tasted good. Lingering sweetness and something that was undefinably *him*. She wound her arms around his neck and lifted closer with a little whimper as the kiss deepened. He grunted against her lips and what had been a slow and easy exploration exploded into something far more heated.

He kissed harder, their tongues working faster against each other, his fingers digging into her back, possessive and hot. The world started to spin and tilt, her senses overwhelmed by him and what her body did in response to his touch.

She was tingling, an achy, glorious feeling that warmed every sensitive part of her. She found herself lifting against him, trying to get closer, trying to find a space where she could feel every inch of him because that was what she was driven to do now. She never wanted his mouth to leave her body—she wanted him to drag it all over her. She was weightless and shaky and needy as he slowly moved her across the room, toward the settee.

When he lowered onto the cushions, pressing a knee in beside her, rocking forward to partially cover her as his fingers glided up her face, against the nape of her neck, she gasped. God, the press of him, the weight of him against her. It was heavenly.

"Roarke," she murmured against his mouth, and he groaned in response, like hearing his name was too much.

He pulled away and his eyes glittered as he got to his feet. He shook his head. "I…can't do this."

Roarke saw how much his refusal hurt Flora and added that to his list of things to hate himself for. It was becoming impossibly long. He felt like he was spinning now, wrong and right blurring together, becoming confusing and impossible to separate.

All he knew was that he wanted this woman, desperately, and it had nothing to do with his cousins and their horrible demands.

She got up from the settee and backed away, blinking rapidly, like she was trying to quell tears. "I-I understand."

"I'm sure you don't," he murmured.

She shook her head and her words fell from her mouth in a rush. "Of course I do. After all, I have little experience—I'm certain I couldn't please a man like you. I don't know what I'm doing. How in the world could I expect to seduce you?"

His eyebrows lifted. "You…you want to seduce me?" he repeated, hating that this was the same verbiage his cousins had used when they made their demands of him. Hearing it from her was a very different experience.

She flushed almost purple and lifted her hands to her cheeks like she was trying to cool them. "Oh Lord, I sound like a fool. I just…it's fine. It's fine that you don't want me. I should just go. Or…it's my house, so I should let you go and…"

He couldn't let her go on like that, thinking that he'd pulled away because he didn't want her. That was the most foolish thing he'd ever heard in his life.

He moved forward and caught her elbow, pulling her closer so he could kiss her again. She made a little murmur of pleasure and tilted her head, deepening the kiss, her tongue exploring him gently, then with more drive and desire.

And he was drowning in her. Drowning in the lightness that filled his chest as she touched him. It was like his problems bled away and there was only her. How long had it been since he felt that way?

It was remarkable.

He drew back and rested his forehead against hers, their panting breaths matching after a few seconds. "It's not about not wanting you," he insisted.

He struggled, trying to find the words to say now. She would certainly hate him even more when he told her he'd kissed her, manhandled her and, oh, by the way, he was doing so partially at the behest of her stepchildren who despised and wanted to harm her. That would destroy any positive feelings she might have about this encounter.

"You want me?" she asked, and the tiny plaintive quality of her voice stopped him short.

She didn't believe she could be wanted. He realized it in a flash of a moment. This woman, this glorious, amazing, fascinating, sweet woman didn't see herself as an object of desire. She didn't understand that he had thought of nothing but her since the moment they'd met. That his erotic dreams had starred her and only her for over a week.

How he hated that she didn't understand that. He nodded. "God help me, Flora, I want you. And if I could—"

She grabbed his hand with both of hers. "You can," she interrupted. She stared up at him, blue eyes shining with anticipation and need and a thousand nuances of pleasure and pain.

And he wanted her. Just for a moment he wanted to fill himself with her scent and her taste and her light and take the tiny glimpse of peace that he saw shining on her face.

Could he do that? Could he separate what he'd been told to do here with her and what he wanted to do? His cousins wanted ruination, he just wanted pleasure.

Could he have one without the other? Give her one without the other?

Yes. There were ways. Technicalities, perhaps, but ones he would cling to if it meant he could have this stolen moment that he suddenly needed as much as his next breath.

"Just a little, Flora," he whispered as he dragged his thumb across her lower lip, felt her surge toward him. "Just for a moment."

~

Flora didn't know what Roarke meant, but it didn't matter. All that mattered was that he brought his mouth back to hers, dragging her flush against him so she could feel the full weight of his desire.

She moved then, guiding them back to the settee. She wanted to feel him without having to focus on remaining upright. They returned to their original positions there, and it was like they'd never stopped.

He glided his lips away from hers, feathering her jawline with kisses and then the column of her throat. She hissed out a breath as sensation increased. God, that felt good. She dropped her head back against the cushions, dragging her fingers into his hair as he sucked gently.

Between her legs she began to throb and she groaned again. She shamelessly and wantonly wanted him there. She wanted to feel his body press against hers, but with no clothing to separate them. She wanted to feel him take a place between her thighs and claim what felt so empty and needy.

She wanted him to become her lover and make her feel this way over and over again. She wanted him to unleash everything he knew on her and then feel him lose control because he was as overwhelmed as she was by the power of their connection.

"Please," she whispered as his mouth moved along the neckline of her silk gown.

He hesitated, lifting his eyes to her. She saw his uncertainty, return some kind of gentlemanly demand that said he couldn't do this. Shouldn't. That it was wrong.

"Please," she repeated, a bit more strenuously. "I want you to."

He shut his eyes and drew a shaky breath. He didn't ask for clarification of what she meant. She supposed it was clear enough with her lifting her hips against him and mewling her pleasure like a cat in heat.

"I don't want to hurt you," he murmured.

She shook her head. "But you wouldn't be. I have nothing to lose, Roarke. I've never wanted something...*someone* so much as I do right now. So if you want me, even just a little, I'm giving you my permission, my consent, to take what you want."

She thought she heard him mutter a curse beneath his breath and he stared down at her body as he let his hands slide down her sides. He gripped her hips, sliding his thumbs along the curves, and she caught her breath. God, whenever, wherever he touched her, it was like he left a mark. She felt the imprint of him across her skin and in her blood.

"When was the last time you...you came?" he asked, glancing back up.

She blinked. She knew what he meant by the question. Orgasm, release. She'd experienced it before, a few times with Stuart, a few more at her own hand. Heat filled her cheeks. "Er, a while. Months?"

He stared. "Months?"

She nodded. "Yes." She barely managed to get the word out.

"Do you want to come?" he pressed, the pressure of his fingers becoming more insistent against her hips, then down across to her thighs. She shivered.

"Y-Yes," she gasped.

His expression softened, but there was still hesitation in his eyes. Like he knew he was doing the wrong thing, no matter what she told him to the contrary.

"I don't have to take," he murmured, she felt like more to himself. "I don't have to steal."

She wanted to say something, to tell him that he wasn't stealing what she freely offered. But he didn't allow her to speak. He pushed forward, kissing her again, cutting off her words and her breath and any cogent thoughts she could have formed.

The kiss felt different now. Like he had a purpose. A drive. His hands moved over her as he sucked her tongue lightly, as he swirled and nipped and tasted her into a pleasure fog. His hands moved as he did so, cupping her thigh, squeezing it as her eyes rolled back in her head and her hands started to shake.

She felt him bunching her skirt with one hand, his fingers catching and raising the fabric around her hips. She forced herself to look down, to watch him reveal her calves, her knees, her thighs and then the garters that held her stockings.

It had been a very long time since someone saw her like this. And Roarke's expression was far more hungry, feral, than Stuart's had ever been.

"You're so pretty," Roarke murmured as he eased himself off the settee, on his knees before her. He widened her legs a fraction—she didn't resist when he did. "I would do such things to you."

Her husband had never talked to her while he touched her. He was gentle, he tended to her needs, he never hurt her, but he had always seemed almost apologetic about his attentions. Like he was trying to work in haste so she wouldn't be troubled too long.

But Roarke was very different. He looked quite wicked there on his knees, his pupils dilated with lust, his hands still gripping around the edge of her drawers, stroking the bare skin between her stocking top and the silky fabric.

He leaned in and his mouth traced the same patch of exposed skin. She bucked at the unexpected electric response of pleasure that his tongue created. Her skin felt alive when he touched it, it tingled in response to the sensation of his mouth on her.

She wanted more.

He fingered the soft fluttering edge of her drawers. "May I take these off?"

He would see her then, half-naked, splayed out like a wanton. She should have been embarrassed by that idea. Instead she was excited.

She nodded and he glided his hands beneath her bunched skirt to find the waistband of her drawers. He untied the little loop of fabric that held them in place and then tugged. She lifted her hips, almost hypnotized by him and his intense focus. He pulled the fabric down her hips, her thighs, and leaned back to pull it entirely away and set them on the floor in a pile.

He wedged himself back between her legs and shivered as he stared at her. Heat filled her cheeks, both the heat of desire and of embarrassment. He was seeing her in the most intimate way, his hands gripped against her thighs, her sex splayed open for his perusal.

"So, so pretty," he whispered, his voice catching. He glanced up at her, examining her face as closely as he examined her most private areas. "I know it's been a while since someone saw you like this. I hope I'm going to make it worth the wait. I want to lick you, Flora. I want to put my mouth here..." He trailed off and gently brushed the tip of his index finger across her entrance.

She lifted against him with a whimper. That little light touch was not enough and it set her on fire for more.

"I'm going to suck you and tease you and make you come." He

leaned up a little on his arms, making his face even with hers again. "But you can tell me no. Now or any time. You can always tell me no."

Her breath caught as she stared into his green eyes. At first she had been afraid of her desire for this man. She'd been afraid of asking for what she wanted. But right now there was something else she feared as she stared into the depths of him and felt something in her…hitch.

What if she ended up more than liking him? What if she wanted more than his hands and mouth on her, then his body inside of hers? What if she lost herself entirely to this man?

Was she prepared for that? Was she guarded against it? Would she know when it was safe to welcome it? And would he ever feel the same if she were so foolish as to fall?

She shook those thoughts off. They were questions for another day. Instead, she cupped his cheek, letting her fingers play along the harsh line of his jaw, and then she tugged him a little closer and kissed him.

He made a muffled sound into her lips but then broke away, and now his gaze was fire. Dangerous and feral. She shivered as he shifted to go back between her legs. He pushed her wider, opening her up in what felt an almost lewd display. And yet she couldn't stop staring as he dropped his head and rubbed his cheek against her inner thigh.

The rasp of the hint of whiskers against her sensitive flesh stole her breath and she gripped the edge of the settee with both hands like she could somehow find purchase there against the rising tide of desire. He smiled up at her and then lifted his mouth to her sex.

It was a closed-mouth kiss at first, gentle, almost gentlemanly if he hadn't been burrowed between her legs in such a shocking way. But all that quickly changed when he made a low grumble against her and his tongue darted out to trace her. She gasped, lifting slightly to meet him, the powerful sensations ripping through her in ways she'd never experienced before.

He glided his hands up her thighs, then used his thumbs to spread her outer lips, massaging until she trembled with pleasure. His tongue went back to tormenting, he circled it around her clitoris slowly, taunting and tasting. She wanted more, she wanted something she couldn't even name when her mind was addled with this intimate exploration.

"Please," she murmured.

He glanced up at her, eyes fire and heat and promises she longed for him to keep. "Yes," he murmured, the reverberation of his words like electric sensation across her sensitive body.

He went back to work at her, but something had shifted. He didn't tease anymore, no, he was focused. He took long, slow licks across her entire entrance, then sucked her clitoris, back and forth for what felt like forever, but could have only been a heated moment or two. He continued to massage her outer lips, perfect pressure that made the heat in her body rise, that made the tingles between her legs shift to more and more intense pleasure.

So when he moved all his attention to the hard nub of her clitoris, stoking and sucking, creating a rhythm that he never altered from, she moved from edgy to on the edge with a terrifying speed. She ground her hips upward, meeting him on every stroke, biting her lip so she wouldn't call down the house with her rising pleasure.

His fingers dug into the flesh of her hips, holding her steady, and he watched her, pupils dilated to almost entirely black as he waited, worked, brought her to the edge of madness and then, with a swirl of his talented tongue, threw her over it.

She let out one soft cry before she clapped her hand over her mouth, muffling the sounds of her pleasure. And oh, there was pleasure. Long, slow waves of it, washing over her, drowning her, changing her forever. He never ceased his torment as she rode them all, just kept sucking and licking her until the pleasure ran right up to the edge of pain and she jerked uncontrollably with her release.

At last she went weak against the cushions, her breath short and hard. He pressed one last kiss to her slick body and then grabbed for the drawers he'd discarded on the floor what felt like a different lifetime ago. He gently helped her get them up her body, tied them beneath her skirt and then smoothed the layers of silk back down. So it looked like he'd never done this to her.

So she looked like she was still the same person, even though she felt very different now.

She swallowed hard. "I…that was remarkable."

He chuckled, a low rough sound and pushed to his feet. "Remarkable is a fine compliment. I tend to agree, *you* are remarkable, Flora."

She sat up a little straighter. "Aren't you going to…that is, won't you…don't you want to…"

He arched a brow. "Take you?"

She nodded, heat flooding her cheeks. "Y-Yes. Take me."

A shiver moved through his whole body. "You don't know how much I want to do just that. But your pleasure is my pleasure today, Your Grace. And I will live on that for a very long time to come."

She tilted her head. A man who only cared for her pleasure? That sounded like a dream in some ways. Only she didn't feel content with the answer. She wanted him to want more. To ask for more. To feel his control break and know she had done that.

"It meant something to me," she said. "What you did. What I felt. It meant a great deal to me. I never thought I'd be wanted again, let alone by…by someone like you."

He stared. "Someone like me?"

"Young, handsome…desirable. I stopped seeing myself as the object of a man's desire a long time ago. So if this is the only time we'll do this, I want you to know that it meant something to me. Thank you." Her cheeks heated as she said those words. It felt so foolish. She pushed to her feet and smoothed her wrinkled skirt. "You—you said before that you had something you wanted to tell me. What is it?"

He opened and shut his mouth for a moment and then shook his head. "Nothing. It was nothing. Just an excuse to come visit you."

"Oh." She bent her head. "Well, I'm glad you did."

"But now we've been locked up in this room for too long." He motioned to the door. "I should go before I can't resist you at all. Will you walk me out onto the drive to wait for my horse?"

She nodded and followed him from the room, but she had an uncomfortable feeling in her chest as she did so. He had done nothing but tend to her desires and make her feel safe and wanted. And yet now as they stood together on the drive, her footman rushing to fetch his mount, she had the uneasy sensation that he wasn't being fully truthful with her. That he was leaving for some other reason than that the time had merely grown too long.

But she wasn't certain how to ask him for more information, to demand he tell her the truth about why his gaze held on hers then moved away over and over again. Because she feared what she'd learn would hurt, and she didn't want to hurt. Not now when she still tingled from his touch. No, she wanted to stay in this fantasy land. At least for a while longer.

In the thirty years that Roarke had been on this planet, he had never felt so torn by opposite emotions as he did standing beside Flora, waiting for his horse to be brought around. The first emotion was easy: desire. He had been free to touch and please her and his world was still shaken. He wanted this woman, and when he was with her he all but forgot the troubles in his life, which was a rare and beautiful thing he didn't want to consider overly much.

Probably because of the *other* emotion that tormented him.

Guilt. He felt awash in guilt. He'd come here meaning to confess his relationship to her stepchildren, to tell her about the threat to her and his role in that thread. But once she'd touched him, kissed him, asked him for more he had been swept away.

And when she'd told him what those moments meant to her, he hadn't been able to crush them with the truth. Which was why he was so bent on running away. He didn't want to take that joyful moment from her. He didn't want to tell her that he had pursued her, at least at first, with an ulterior motive.

His horse was almost here now, he could see the footman drawing him around the corner. In a few moments he would be able to ride away, regroup, find some other mode of confession or protection for Flora.

Only before the animal had arrived, up the lane rode Callum. He stopped at the house just next to Flora's where Valaria lived, and smiled over at Flora and Roarke.

"Good afternoon!" he called out as he handed over his own reins and came down to Flora's door. "What a pleasure to see you two. Have you been calling, Roarke?"

Flora shifted, her hands clenched in front of her. "We were just talking," she burst out.

Callum lifted both brows at the strenuousness of her tone. "Er, very good. Well, I was just about to join Valaria for a late tea. Why don't you two come down and join us?"

Flora glanced over at Roarke, her gaze seeking his. "You...you needn't if you have someplace else to be."

Roarke heard the lilt of hope in her tone. And he saw Callum's judgment of his response. Worse yet he felt the call to stay. To spend a little more time with her in a way that would further buffer what they'd just done together from what he would ultimately have to tell her about himself.

"I'd be pleased to join you," he found himself saying. Meaning it, too. After all, if he didn't have this wretched secret hanging over himself, if he had nothing to stop him, he would have been only pleased to spend more time with this woman and their friends.

And perhaps that was unfair of him to want to have that moment. But he intended to take it.

CHAPTER 11

Valaria was just as welcoming to the pair as Callum had been, and soon they found themselves a cozy foursome, seated out on Valaria's veranda in the rare warmth of the autumn day. The leaves were turning, fluttering reds and oranges on the light breeze.

Roarke glanced at Flora. He could still taste her on his lips. No amount of tea could erase that flavor of her passion. He didn't want it to. He wanted to hold that moment close, not sully it with what would eventually come.

She was laughing now at something Valaria had said. The two women had their heads close together as they chatted and he was fascinated by how comfortable Flora was with her friends. There was none of the hesitance in this space, none of the belief that she could not earn welcome the way she feared she would not earn his desire.

"I think Callum and I will get a dog once we're married," Valaria was saying with a wink for the duke.

Callum smiled with indulgence and glanced at Roarke. "She thinks she can make me fall head over heels in love with a puppy. And she's likely right. She knows she just has to crook her finger and I'll fall right in line."

Roarke couldn't help but be moved at the warmth between his friend and the duchess. They seemed truly in love and it was nice to see Callum so happy. They had a future laid out before them once Valaria's official mourning period was over, an easy joy that was right here and would only grow in the future. He was almost jealous of it, and tried not to look at Flora with those thoughts in his head.

"When I married Stuart, he had five dogs, all ancient things that puttered around the house like little old men," Flora said with a laugh. "But it was all a ruse, meant to trick me."

"The dogs were playing a trick on you?" Roarke asked, leaning forward. "How so?"

"One day I decided we all needed some exercise, an escape from..." She trailed off and shook her head. "I needed air. And I took these five old man dogs out with me for a short walk in the garden. Well, apparently this wasn't done without a lead, which I didn't know, because the moment we exited the confines of the pathways, they realized they were free and started *running*."

Roarke laughed. "I thought they were old putterers."

"So did I!" Flora said, smiling as Callum and Valaria laughed, too. "Here I am, gathering up my skirts, racing after these five demons in disguise as dogs, screeching their names in rapid succession: Anton, Ruby, Fierce, Bottle, Dragon!" She glanced at Roarke. "Before you start, I didn't name them."

He chuckled again at her story. "I would never judge the serious name of a serious dog, Your Grace."

"Well, we reached the top of the hill behind the estate, and I lost my footing and tumbled, just rolled down this hill, still shouting for the dogs all the way down." She shook her head, eyes lit up with mirth. "Somehow I managed not to break or bruise anything beyond my pride. But my tumble caught their attention, and as I sit up, covered in grass and dirt, here come five now filthy dogs racing back and they just all crowd on top of me, licking and bouncing."

"Oh no!" Valaria gasped, holding her sides from laughter. "Did you manage to get them back up to the house?"

"I suppose they took pity on me and followed me back up. I came into the foyer and Stuart was passing through and looked me up and down. I told him what happened and he said, *Oh yes, no one trusts those dogs, Flora.* Then he patted each of their heads and they waddled off after him, back to being old men."

Flora had done an impression of his uncle's voice and it made Roarke laugh even harder because it was remarkably spot on.

"Did you ever take them out in the garden without leads again?" he asked.

She nodded. "Of course! I saw how happy they were to be free, and I did it all the time after that." She sighed. "They were excellent dogs, if a bit crafty."

They all laughed again and once again, Roarke basked in the warmth of Flora's light, of her kindness and sweetness, her humor. Sometimes it felt as though he had a constant pressure on his chest, a persistent reminder of his failures and responsibilities. But here with her, he didn't feel it quite so keenly. He might not deserve that respite, but it felt like a balm on his soul.

He cleared his throat and shifted his attention toward Valaria, who he found already watching him like a hawk. "You have a lovely home, Valaria."

"Thank you," she said with a slight incline of her head. It was evident by the way she was always watching and reading him that she didn't fully trust his motives. He deserved that, of course. "Since we've just been talking of gardens, what do you think of mine, Mr. Desmond?"

He blinked. While Flora's story had involved a garden, they hadn't really been talking *about* a garden. "Er, it's quite lovely."

They all looked out over the area in question. Of course, it was fall now and much of the beauty was muted with the leaves fallen and flowers deadheaded and ready for their winter rest.

"Perhaps you'd like to walk in it," Valaria said. "I'll show you my roses."

He blinked. The dead roses? And yet she didn't truly seem to be requesting he join her, but demanding it. "I'm sure that would be pleasant."

Flora had started to shift in her chair when Valaria turned her sharp expression on him, and now she leaned forward. "What a lovely idea for all of us. We could walk—"

Valaria lifted a hand. "Oh no, I think Callum wished to speak to you about something, Flora. Mr. Desmond and I can take this little jaunt together while you do that." She stood. "Come now."

He stood because there was no denying her, it seemed, and followed the duchess to the edge of the veranda where a short set of stone stairs led to the garden below. At the top he looked back to find Flora watching with a concerned expression on her face, which did nothing to quell his own nervousness.

But the duchess didn't launch into an attack, at least at first. They walked together through her brown garden, the cool autumn breeze stirring against his face. Finally, Valaria stopped and pivoted to face him. "I don't know how to be anything but direct anymore, Mr. Desmond. What are your intentions with my friend?"

He blinked. "Er, yes, that *is* direct," he said with a nervous laugh.

"Well, I must be," she said, and shrugged. "Flora deserves the world. And she has few people on her side. Her husband's dreadful family would destroy her if they could find a way."

He flinched as he thought of his cousins and their cruel intentions toward her. He hadn't meant to outwardly show that, but Valaria immediately arched a brow.

"Has she told you about them?" she asked. "You seem to know."

He nodded. "Er, yes. I know about her stepchildren. I know about their cruelty."

She seemed surprised, but to his relief she didn't pursue his knowledge about his cousins. Instead she folded her arms. "So what do you want, Mr. Desmond?"

He cleared his throat. That question sparked a hundred images for him. His mother, his hovel of a home, his having to beg his cousins for basic human decency…yes, he saw all those things flow through his mind. But he also saw Flora. Her smile, her bright gaze in the museum, her mouth turned up toward his, her body shuddering against his tongue.

"I don't want to hurt her," he said softly.

Valaria nodded. "Do you like her?"

There was no hesitation in how he answered then. "Yes," he said. "Anyone who doesn't is a fool. She is a remarkable woman."

He shifted as he realized he'd repeated the compliment he'd given her after their encounter a short time before. When she'd still been shaky with pleasure. When he'd tried to step away from her for his own good. For hers.

"Well, that's very good," Valaria said. "It's an excellent start, at any rate, that you can see her value. But I must tell you, Mr. Desmond—Roarke—that if you do hurt her, I'll be certain someone hurts you."

His eyes grew wide at that promise, said with a sweet smile. The lady was not in jest. It was a promise she made, not a threat. And he admired her for it. "I would deserve it," he said.

"Good, then that's settled," Valaria said. "We understand each other. Would you like to look at the fountain? Flora says you are a lover of art and it's really a wonderful piece."

"Yes," he said, and offered his arm, which she took this time. "Why don't you lead the way?"

Flora leaned as far as she could over the veranda wall without falling and twisted around to find Valaria and Roarke walking through the half-dead gardens together.

"She looks very intense," she said before she glanced at Callum. He was still seated at the table, leaning back in his chair, entirely unbothered. "Oh God, what do you think they're saying?"

The inspired a chuckle in her companion. "Valaria is probably threatening him if he ever were to hurt you."

Flora felt the color leave her cheeks and she took a long step toward Callum. "She wouldn't!"

"Of course she would," Callum said. "After what she endured? She would go to war to protect anyone she cared about from ever going through pain. That singular dedication to safeguarding those she loves is one of her greatest qualities." He shook his head. "Won't you sit down? You're making me dizzy spinning around to look at them and then back to me and then back to them again."

Flora let out her breath and stomped back to her place at the table. She took it gingerly and glanced over her shoulder. "I do appreciate Valaria for her steadfast friendship, but this is humiliating. Roarke doesn't deserve this much attention from her. He and I aren't anything to each other."

She couldn't help but think of him on his knees, perched between her thighs, watching her as she twisted in pleasure against him. She could feel her face becoming red with the thought.

Callum arched a brow. "From that blush, I feel like you might be lying to me, Flora."

She tossed her napkin toward him with a huff of breath. "It is so entirely ungentlemanly of you to point that out."

He laughed again. "Very much so, my deepest apologies." His smile faded as he reached across the table and took her hand for the briefest of squeezes. "My dear Flora, please know that we all only want to see you happy."

"I'd also like to be happy," Flora admitted. "I just...don't know if I remember how."

Callum's brow wrinkled. "I know Roarke a little. He's always seemed upstanding. Would it make you more comfortable if I looked into him a bit more? Gave you some information beyond what I recall from a boyhood acquaintance and whatever he presents to the world now?"

Her breath stopped at that idea. Perhaps that would help her find her bearings, if she knew more about Roarke. Even if she didn't feel good about going behind his back for any information. "Yes," she whispered.

"Then I will," Callum promised. "And please know you can always reach out to me about this man or any man who darkens your door. You are like Valaria's sister, which means in a few months that you will be my sister. And I will do anything I can to be certain you are safe and happy."

Flora stared at him, this handsome man who she already knew was a magnificent steward to her friend's heart. This kind gesture warmed her own. Made her feel…loved. Not in a passionate way, but like a family. She had been missing that for so long.

"You are too kind," she whispered, and then looked back again, toward where Roarke and Valaria had last been seen. "Now can we go after them before she scares him off?"

Callum grinned as he got up and offered an arm. "Of course," he said.

She took his offering and allowed him to guide her down the stone stairs and across the garden to where she could now see Roarke and Valaria standing at her empty fountain, admiring the statue of Artemis that decorated it.

"You know," Callum said just before they reached the pair. "If he could be scared off, he truly doesn't deserve you."

She smiled up at him before she let him go. "You really are the best of men. And you and Valaria deserve all your happiness to come."

He released her and crossed to Valaria, taking her arm gently. "We could not wait for your return, my love."

Valaria sent Flora a knowing look, but if she had been haranguing Roarke, he didn't look any worse for wear for it. He seemed entirely unbothered, even as he tracked Flora when she stepped closer.

"It has been a wonderful afternoon," he said. "And I am so glad we bumped into you, Callum, when I was departing Flora's estate.

But I truly must continue my day, as much as I hate to leave the company."

"I'll walk you back to home," Flora said. "And we can say our goodbyes."

Valaria drew a breath like she was going to say something, but Callum tucked an arm around her waist and gave her a gentle squeeze. "I'm sure we'll see you later, Flora. And always good to see you, Desmond."

Roarke inclined his head and the group of them headed around the path through the garden to the gate that led to the front drive. Valaria and Callum waved them off and after a few steps Flora was alone with Roarke again.

"I hope she wasn't too…too hard on you."

He smiled down at her. "She's protective. That's a lovely quality in a friend."

"Yes, I'm lucky to have her and Bernadette." They had reached her small stable by then and she waved at the stablehand. He nodded and went for Roarke's horse.

She stared up at Roarke and oh, how she wanted to kiss him. But she'd used up all her bravado earlier in the day with her seduction that had ended with such pleasure.

"Will I…will I see you again?" she asked, and hoped she didn't sound as desperate as she felt.

There was a moment when she saw what looked like panic cross his expression and her heart leapt with fear. Perhaps all he wanted was what they'd already done. Perhaps all of it was out of pity, not true desire. Oh, how that would break her heart.

"I…" he began, and then he smiled, his expression softening, his gaze becoming more focused on her. "What about tomorrow? I could meet you in the park and we could walk together."

The relief and excitement that lifted through her chest and into her entire body was so strong that she couldn't deny how much this man's company was beginning to mean to her. She tempered it, trying to maintain some calm as she said, "I would enjoy that. How about around one? Then we could have tea after if you have time."

"I'll see you at one."

The horse was ready now and Roarke took the reins from her servant with a smile. Once the man had gone, Roarke took her hand and lifted it to his lips. She wasn't wearing gloves, so the warmth of his lips eased through her skin and made her weak in the knees. He met her gaze as he kissed her skin, the promise in his eyes bold and passionate.

"I very much look forward to that, Flora."

Then he swung up on his mount and rode away, leaving her to stare after him, with a hundred memories to relive until they met again.

CHAPTER 12

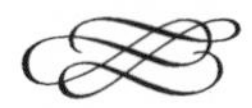

Roarke had grown up in a fine townhouse, not unlike Flora's, with a handful of servants and access to almost anything he might have wanted. Over the years, as his father's fortune had slipped, the family had slumped lower into smaller homes, fewer servants, possessions and clothing that were more worn and out of fashion.

And once Roarke had mishandled what little fortune he'd inherited after his father's death? Well, that had landed him in his current accommodations. A hovel was a kind description. It was a single tiny room above a smoky pub on a street he hadn't even known existed as a young man. And while it was safe and nearly warm and almost always dry except when rain blew against the windows from a certain direction, it was not fine. It was not a place he would bring friends or, God forbid, a lover.

He tried to picture Flora here, her sunshine lighting all the darkest corners. But all he could see was the horror on her face if she knew where he stayed. Worse, what he was.

A liar.

He'd meant to tell her the truth yesterday. At least, he'd believed he had. But the moment she started talking about seduction and desire, the moment she'd kissed him, he'd just let all the bad things float away. He'd let himself have the tiniest taste of happiness for the first time in a very long time.

And now he hated himself even more for it.

"I will do it today," he told the grainy reflection of himself in the cracked mirror where he was looking to get himself into acceptable condition to meet Flora for their walk. "I'll tell her, as gently as possible." He bent his head. God, what could he say?

"Flora," he said to the mirror image. "I lied to you. I was sent here by your stepchildren."

God, he could almost imagine her expression crumpling with pain and hurt and hate. The hate was what he dreaded most. He'd have earned it with his ungentlemanly behavior. No amount of practiced words would change the meaning of what he'd have to say to her.

There was a rap on the door behind him and he frowned at it. Probably his landlady. She always banged on the door like she was ready to tear it off its hinges.

"Mrs. Westin," he said as he came to it, opening it. "My rent is not due for—" He cut himself off. It wasn't his grizzled-faced landlady who stood there waiting for him. It was his cousin, Philip.

He looked almost enraptured as he peered past Roarke into the home. His pleasure in the face of pain was so complete it made Roarke despise his cousin even more. A pure hatred rose in him and he stepped to the side to block the view.

"What do you want?" he snapped.

Philip chuckled before he shoved past Roarke and into the room. "That's not a very polite way to speak to the man who holds your purse strings."

"The duke holds the purse strings, Philip," Roarke snapped. "You're just the lackey."

It was probably imprudent to say so, and Philip's enraged expression verified that. But then his cousin drew a few deep breaths, his fists relaxed at his sides and he looked around. "Good

Lord, this place is utter shite. Your part of the family was never exactly dripping in gold, but you truly have fallen."

Roarke lifted his chin and tried not to let the vulnerability he felt in this moment overtake him. He didn't let people see this life he was forced to lead exactly because of this judgment.

"My mother gets the lion's share of whatever funds I manage to scrape together," he said. "Which I know you know since you and your siblings are lording her safety over me."

Philip smiled as he drew a gloved fingertip over the surface of a table. But Roarke kept the small space clean, so he had no satisfaction in finding dust or debris left behind.

"We use what we can," Philip said. "It worked, didn't it? After all, I know you saw Flora yesterday."

Roarke stared at him, his stomach turning. "Thomas had me fucking followed?"

"Well, we're not certain we can fully trust you, cousin," Philip said, and looked up at him, his smile cold and brittle. "Perhaps I misjudged you, though. Our man said he saw you two standing very close together at the stable there, and that you…" His voice dropped, became huskier. "...kissed her hand."

Roarke staggered back. That moment by his horse had felt so personal, so private. He could still feel the weight of Flora's fingers against his. That had been real, not a manipulation, just like the time they'd shared in her parlor had been real.

And now it was spoiled because he knew Thomas had been watching it all, through his proxy. Perhaps even through Philip, himself. That his cousins had been judging and laughing and seeing it as a way to hurt Flora.

"I'm working on it," Roarke ground out through clenched teeth. "These things take time."

The taunting pleasure of Philip's expression faded and a hardness entered his eyes. He leaned closer. "Working on it?" he repeated with a shake of his head. "That sounds like an excuse. Sort of like how so many things in your pathetic life have been an excuse. Are the stakes not high enough, cousin? Because Thomas has given me permission to make them higher."

"What are you talking about?" Roarke asked.

"Your mother's caretaker seems a lovely woman. Married, has two children."

Now Roarke's breath shortened. "Leave my mother alone."

"She's quite unwell, isn't she? My dear aunt, your sweet mother. I cannot imagine how hard it would be for her if she lost the support of the woman who is her constant companion."

Roarke drew back. "You're...you're threatening my mother's servant?"

"My brother says we could pay her off to walk away." Philip shrugged. "But there are other ways to make her leave. Whatever happens, I don't think you could take care of your mother here. Especially when you lose all your incoming funds."

"You've made your threats clear enough already," Roarke hissed.

"Not clear enough, obviously," Philip said. "When will it be done?"

Roarke stared at him, this monster who shared some small portion of his blood. This cruel person who was so focused on hurting Flora that he didn't care who he destroyed in the meantime. There would be no stopping him.

"I'm seeing her today," Roarke said flatly.

For a moment, Philip's rage grew bright again. Then he nodded. "Excellent. Move it along. We want it done before the time runs out on the inheritance clock."

He pivoted then and left without so much as a goodbye for Roarke. When he was alone again, Roarke sank into his chair before the fire and covered his face. He was in an untenable situation now. One he couldn't escape. Hurt Flora or hurt his mother. Either way, he would be destroyed.

And he had no idea what to do now.

~

Flora felt like she was floating as she entered the park across from Kent's Row for her meeting with Roarke. She had been pacing her home all day, watching the clock, lamenting how long every minute took to tick by. But now she felt free as she breathed in the cool autumn air and looked around for this man who had taken such a big role in her life as of late.

She found him almost immediately, coming across the park from the opposite entrance. Even from a distance, she recognized him, there was something about the way he moved. But as he got closer, her smile faltered. Was there something wrong? His shoulders looked slightly slumped, and when he caught sight of her as he got closer, his mouth got tight before he lifted his hand and waved. She waved back and crossed to meet him.

"Good afternoon, Flora," he said, his voice a little rough.

"Good afternoon," she said back. "We've been lucky with the weather the past few days. I'm so pleased we can walk now, as it looks like a storm will be coming soon."

He looked up at the gathering gray clouds in the distance and nodded. "Indeed. Well, let's walk, shall we?"

He offered his arm and she took it, reveling in the awareness the simple touch awoke in her. She had been dreaming of touching this man since yesterday and now it felt like a relief to do so.

They walked along the path for a little while in silence. She wished she could say an amenable silence, a comfortable one, but the farther they went, the less easy it became. Roarke sometimes glanced at her then looked away. His mouth was drawn and taut.

"Is there something wrong, Roarke?" she asked at last.

He jerked his gaze toward her. "Why would you say that?"

"I just noticed a few things," she said carefully. "Your expression is not especially happy at present and you seem troubled in the way you're walking."

His brows lifted. "The way I'm walking," he repeated.

She nodded. "Shorter steps, too fast, you're certainly not

enjoying a stroll. It feels more like you're going to the gallows. So I wondered if something had happened to trouble you."

He stopped and stared off in the distance, then shook his head. "Are you always so aware of those around you, Your Grace?"

She worried her lip. "With those I…I care about, certainly."

Now he pivoted toward her fully and looked down into her face. There was something so sad about his expression now. Something that spoke of hurt. "And you count me as one of those people."

"I like you," she admitted slowly. Softly. "I assume you knew that after yesterday. I don't normally go around surrendering myself to just anyone."

He nodded, though his mouth got even tighter. "It's complicated," he said. "And I know that I need to tell you about it. Tell you everything. But I dread what will happen afterward."

She swallowed. "I'm not sure what that means, Roarke, but I want to help if I can. Even if that is just being an ear to tell your story to. Sometimes that means the most." She took his hand in both of hers, loving the weight of it between her palms, that his fingers were rough against her softer skin. "Come back to my house," she suggested. "We'll have our tea a little early and you can tell me anything you'd like. Everything you need to say. And I promise that I'll listen and offer whatever support I can."

"You would," he whispered. "That's just who you are, isn't it? Down to your very core, down to that beating heart." He drew in a long breath. "Yes, let's go back to your home. And I'll tell you everything."

She took his arm and they started back across the park. She should have felt happy that he had agreed to open up to her in this way. She should have been excited about where that could lead for them down the road.

Only there was something in his expression that made her worried. And she couldn't shake the uneasy feeling that everything was about to change.

Roarke sat in Flora's parlor, on the same settee where he had pleasured her the day before, watching her prepare tea for them both. He tried to memorize her face, hold every detail in his mind before she only looked at him with disappointment, anger, hatred. How could she not?

"What happened that troubled you so?" she asked as she handed a cup to him, sweetened as he liked it.

He sipped the brew. He felt an incredible drive to tell her more about himself. To give her something so that once the truth was out at least she'd understand a little about why.

He cleared his throat. "My father was an interesting man," he began.

She tilted her head. "*Interesting* can be a loaded term."

"He was brilliant and creative and caring when he remembered any of us existed. But he was not prudent," he explained, and smiled as he thought of the old man and his certainty that whatever he invested in next would be the biggest return. "And he wasted almost all we had before he died of an apoplexy several years ago."

"I'm sorry," she said, and he could see how much she wanted to touch him. He wished she would. Wished the warmth and light of her would brighten his life one more time. One last time.

"Around the time of his passing, my mother's health began to decline. She had always been flighty, but this was something more. In the last few years she's gotten to the point where she doesn't know where she is most of the time, often doesn't know who I am." He swallowed past a sudden lump in his throat. "I try to take care of her, but I fear I fail. I watch her slipping away and I can't give her everything she might need to make this final time comfortable. Happy, or as happy as I can."

She moved to sit next to him and lifted her hand, wiping a tear from his cheek that he hadn't realized had fallen. He turned into her palm, letting her cup his face, reveling in everything this woman was. Everything she could bring to a life, everything he wished he could ask for in that moment.

Only he couldn't. It wasn't right. It wasn't fair.

"I understand now why you seemed so upset when you arrived in the park today. Why your expression is often so troubled when we're together," Flora said. "I'm so sorry you are enduring that—it must be so difficult."

He nodded and then drew a long breath. "But my reactions to that haven't always been right or fair or good, Flora. I've taken advantage of your sweetness, of your acceptance, and I hate myself for that."

She blinked and lowered her hand. "Are you referring to yesterday? To what happened here in the parlor on the settee?"

"I shouldn't have taken advantage, taken some tiny part of what you offered," he said with a shake of his head. "Not when you didn't know everything. Not when you believed me to be something I wasn't. Am not."

She leaned closer, shifting on the settee so their legs touched. "I *like* what you are, Roarke. More powerfully than I thought was possible. You didn't take anything, not anything I didn't offer."

He opened his mouth to speak, to tell her that wasn't true, but she didn't allow it. She leaned forward and her mouth took his. Yesterday she had been hesitant, explorative when they kissed. He'd taken the lead. But today she seemed more certain. She cupped both his cheeks gently and traced his lips with her tongue.

He couldn't resist her even when he knew he should. When she touched him, it was magic, shutting off everything but her, soothing his deepest pains and making him feel...good. She made him feel *good*. And he selfishly allowed it for a moment, tilting his head so the kiss deepened.

She wound her arms around his neck with a little groan of pleasure, her breasts flattening against his chest. He had no idea how long they sat there, kissing each other, drowning in each other, but he felt the heat of their connection rising. He felt this powerful desire moving toward its natural end.

Taking her. Having her. Claiming her.

He wanted it so much. He wanted to make love to her on the settee, on the floor, to carry her up to her bed, he didn't care where. He just wanted to strip her bare, touch her everywhere, feel her body flex around his as she gasped and cried out his name in pleasure. He wanted to pretend that he wasn't who he was. That he could do all those things and then walk with her in the park and take her to museums and build something that felt like a life when images of it fluttered around the edges of his heated mind.

Only he couldn't. He fought the tide of pleasure her touch created, tried to recall that he wasn't an absolute bastard and he had to pull away. After another moment in her arms, he would pull away.

"Stop touching her!"

The sharp, angry voice at the door startled them apart. Flora pivoted, her face bright with embarrassment, and they both faced the intruder. It was Callum, standing with Theo just behind him. And they both looked very angry.

"Oh no," Flora said, getting up and moving toward them, her hands raised. "I realize what this looks like, but you needn't defend my honor. I wanted this, I—"

"Don't," Theo said softly, taking her hand and drawing her between them as he glared at Roarke. And in that moment he knew that they had uncovered his secret. And they were going to reveal him in this worst possible moment in the worst possible way.

And everything would burn around him.

CHAPTER 13

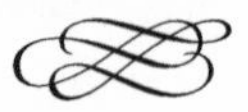

Flora shook her head, still trying to find a way to explain to her two friends, her gallant protectors, that what they had interrupted wasn't something negative. It certainly hadn't felt like that, not at all. Roarke had offered her vulnerability, a glimpse at something devastating in his life. And when she had offered comfort in response it had all made sense.

As did the burning desire that seemed to consume her whenever he was near her. She didn't want that to end. Whether he was her temporary lover or someone who could be more, she wanted to explore that passion without interruption from well-meaning friends.

"You used us to get to her," Theo said, his hands shaking as he continued to half-block Flora like a shield.

Roarke got to his feet slowly. All the color was gone from his cheeks. "Please let me explain."

She had been drawing a breath to defend him, but when he said those words she stopped and stared at him. He didn't look upset or afraid or confused at this interruption. He looked...guilty.

"What do you need to explain?" she croaked, coming around Theo, batting his hand away when he reached for her again, like he could hold her back from whatever was happening here. Protect her.

She realized now, in a burst of horror, that she was likely going to need that protection. From Roarke. A man she had come to trust and desire and…and care about in a way she'd thought she would never feel again.

Roarke drew a breath. "How much do you know?" he asked. The question was directed not at her, but at them. She darted her gaze toward Callum, whose jaw was trembling with rage.

"All of it," he growled. "So there will be no lying around it, Desmond. In fact, just to ensure it, why don't *I* tell her?"

"No," Flora said, moving forward another step. "If there is some secret, some lie to be revealed, I would hear it from Roarke. Please —" She met his eyes again, searching for some kernel of comfort there. Some little thing that would quell her growing fears. But there was none. "Tell me what is going on."

Roarke shook his head. "I told you a little about my—my father today, but I left out one detail. He was…he had sisters, one sister in particular. Her name was Elizabeth. And when she was married, she was known as the…the Duchess of Sidmouth."

The words hit her like daggers and she staggered back a step. Callum caught her elbow and she leaned against him for a brief moment when her legs wouldn't hold her. Elizabeth, the first wife of her late husband. The mother of the stepchildren who despised Flora. The woman whose portrait had glared down at Flora the entire time she'd been married to Stuart.

"That isn't possible," she whispered. "Because if Elizabeth was your aunt, that would mean that you would have…would have known who I was all along. That you would have had some kind of relationship with my husband. That…that…"

"That I was…" Roarke sounded as sick as she now felt. "I was sent here by my cousins, Flora. By your stepchildren to spy on you. And later to seduce you."

The blood rushed to her ears and Flora suddenly could hear

nothing but those horrible words echoing through her head. From what felt like a great distance, she heard Callum cursing at Roarke. Saw through a fog that Theo held him back but was shouting at Roarke just as strenuously.

She forced herself to look at Roarke instead of them. Through the fog, moving in slow motion, his expression was crumpled, filled with regret and guilt and pain. He felt *pain* that this was happening. Even though he had caused it. *He* had done this.

She shook her head and came back into the room fully, the fog lifted. She stepped between the shouting men and Roarke and faced her friends. "I want to talk to him alone."

That stopped Theo and Callum in their tracks. They stared at her for a fraction of a moment. She felt Roarke's gaze on her back, as well, but refused to face him.

"That's not a good idea," Callum said, his tone gentle now.

"No," Theo agreed. "He doesn't deserve to spend time alone with you."

She pivoted and now speared Roarke with a glare. She hoped it looked steadier than she felt. Inside she felt like wobbling jelly. "But *I* deserve the truth. Without witnesses to this further humiliation. I want to talk to him alone. Please, you can wait outside to insure he doesn't do anything."

Roarke's eyebrows lifted at that caveat. His only reaction to her anger. And while she didn't believe he would physically harm her—she knew it in her soul, actually—she had also thought she knew other things about him. To her soul. So perhaps she wasn't the best judge of him, of anyone, even herself.

Callum and Theo exchanged a look and then Callum let out a long breath. "We'll be just outside the door." He gently squeezed her hand and then the two men left, closing the door behind themselves.

She stared after them. Closing the door so she and Roarke could be alone had always been a naughty pleasure, a daring grasp at her own desires. But now…now it was like a jail door slamming.

"Flora," he said behind her, his voice laced with grief and heartache.

She pivoted to look at him, drank him in even now when she was so hurt and confused. "Was anything true?" she whispered.

He caught his breath. "Yes."

She shook her head. He'd said the word she wanted to hear, but now it felt so hollow. "How can I believe you?"

"You can't," he said without hesitation, without excuse. "Not after what you just heard. Not after what more I'll tell you. I don't expect you to believe me. But I will tell you just the same that whatever my purpose was in initially pursuing you, every time we talked or touched or kissed, it was real. So real that I lost myself in it. In you."

Oh, but those words were seductive. So was his expression, and she saw honesty and passion and emotion in his green eyes. And yet she could not be such a fool as to lean into that. "You seem to have every reason to lie, though, don't you?"

He pursed his lips. "I deserve that. But if it wasn't true, then I could have allowed us to be caught at the gallery for a scandal that would please my cousins. I could have taken you on that very settee behind me instead of pulling away when I did. I could have disclosed to my cousins what happened between us instead of telling my family that nothing had transpired."

She shifted. Perhaps all those things were true. But she still didn't understand the motivation. "Why did they send you after me?"

"The additional clause to my uncle's will," he said.

She blinked. "Clause?"

His eyes went wide. "You don't know?"

She shook her head. "The will was resolved years ago. I know nothing else but what was revealed at that time."

"Damn them." He squeezed his eyes shut and took a long breath. "I-I know you received a settlement after his death, but it turns out there was more. If you hadn't remarried or taken a lover by the three-year anniversary of his death, you would get an additional ten thousand pounds."

For a moment it felt like the world had screeched to a halt. She struggled to find her breath. "I-I didn't know."

He bent his head. "Well, they thought you did. They cruelly assumed you would act as they would, and hide any lover you had waiting in the wings in order to collect on the inheritance next month."

She flinched. She hadn't exactly been thinking of the impending anniversary of her loss. For the first time since Stuart's death, actually. This man's doing, and now it was all a lie. Her newfound peace ruined by a few callous actions. "So they sent you to spy?"

"Yes." He looked sick as he said it. "They thought I would uncover that secret lover's identity and they could bring it to the solicitors to void the clause. So I...I investigated you. Followed you."

She heard a broken sound escape her lips and wished she could take it back. She didn't want to show him that vulnerability.

"And yes, I did use my relationship to Callum and Theo in order to meet you."

She shook her head. "It was all a manipulation."

"No," he insisted, and took a step forward.

Oh, how she wanted to fall into him, to receive whatever comfort he would offer. But that time was over now. Instead she stepped back and he stopped his advance with a frown.

"No," he repeated. "I met you and was instantly charmed. Taken in by your very real and true kindness and warmth. I didn't know you weren't aware of the money, but I knew you weren't lying so you could receive it. And I told them that."

Anger swelled in her as she stared at him, full of excuses and seductive words and sentiments. "You act as though you were heroic. But you've already admitted that you also agreed to seduce me so that they would win their blood money back."

He blanched. "Yes. I did that. When I told them that you weren't doing anything wrong, they blackmailed me. I have nothing, Flora. It wasn't just my father who was imprudent. I lost *everything* last year in a terrible investment. I have to beg them for the smallest amount of money just to maintain my mother's small existence. I live in a wretched place I would never subject you or anyone else to. They know all that and they threatened to take everything away. And not only that but to ensure I couldn't even work in order to support her."

She bent her head. If she knew one thing it was that her stepchildren were very capable of such cruelty. She had been the butt of their actions many a time during her marriage. They had always been Stuart's blind spot. He insisted she would one day win his children over and excused their bad behavior.

And here they were, at the ultimate consequence of their unchecked greed and malice.

"I was trapped between protecting my mother and protecting you. And trying to find a way out without harming either one of you. I swear that I intended to tell you today."

She lifted her gaze back to his. "That is mightily convenient. You meant to tell me today, after what happened between us here yesterday, after we were interrupted in a passionate embrace by my friends."

"I know I was wrong," he said, and his voice cracked. "But you don't know how much your company, your light, has meant to me in the few weeks we've known each other, Flora. I was selfish, I wanted to hang on to that for a few more moments."

She stared at him. "Well, you did. You made me a fool in the process. Is there anything else?"

He drew a sharp breath. "They told me that if I could not seduce you myself, they would find someone who would. Whether or not you agreed."

Her stomach dropped. He was talking about Thomas and his

siblings hiring someone to…to…rape her if need be. For a moment, she couldn't help but appreciate that Roarke had taken their devil's bargain. How he'd tried, in however misguided a way, to protect her.

"And did they also offer to pay you?" she whispered.

There was a hesitation that told her the answer even before he whispered, "Five thousand pounds if I succeeded in breaking the inheritance."

For a moment she lost her breath. Five thousand pounds was a fortune. It made her sick not only that her stepchildren had been willing to pay so much just to hurt her, but also that Roarke had agreed to take such a sum for his actions. It made his reflections on his motives all the more suspect.

"Is that all? Is that every secret?" she asked, her voice shaking. She hated that it shook, hated that she revealed herself to him. She didn't want to be vulnerable to him anymore.

"Yes." His voice broke again. "I'm sorry, Flora."

"I'm sure you are, since you won't be receiving anything, after all," she said softly. "I'm also sure you are, since you were caught in your lies rather than getting to find a way to work around them because I was so foolish as to fall under your spell."

"I'm sorry I hurt you," he said. "That I continue to hurt you."

"If there's nothing else for you to add, then you should go," she said, eyes stinging. She wanted him gone before the tears fell. "I don't want to see you again."

He recoiled but didn't argue. "I understand. Please, though, tell me you will be careful. My cousins are cruel beyond measure and they are driven when it comes to this subject."

"That's the worst part, Roarke. If you had come to me from the beginning, if you had explained this was happening after we met, we could have been partners in this problem. We could have worked through it together." She moved toward the parlor door, and there she stopped and turned back to him. "But you didn't. And now I know the truth. And there's nothing else to say." She pulled the door open and motioned for him to go. "Goodbye."

He walked across the room and her breath hitched despite herself. "Goodbye."

He moved past her and she had a wild desire to reach out to touch him one last time. She managed to quell that and instead only watched him depart. And realized that he took some piece of her heart with him.

~

Roarke was numb as he stepped out of Flora's parlor and into the foyer. It was like walking through a nightmare, one he had created and deserved. Callum and Theo were standing there, waiting for him and he tensed, preparing for whatever would come next.

Neither man spoke, but they flanked him as he moved to the front door and out onto the step. Clearly they had already asked for his horse, because it was waiting there for him.

"For what it's worth, I'm sorry," he said softly, daring to look at the two men who he'd begun to consider friends.

Theo shook his head. "You are, indeed. My best advice to you, Mr. Desmond, is not to darken her door again."

He nodded. "I understand. But I would ask—"

"You dare to ask something?" Callum snapped.

"My cousins are driven. Please keep an eye on her. They might not be finished with their attempt to destroy her and take what isn't theirs." He met each man's stare, one after the other. "You may hate me, as does she, and I deserve all of it. But I beg of you to listen to that one request."

Callum's nostrils flared. "She'll be taken care of. Now go."

Roarke slung up on his horse. He nudged him into motion and rode toward the gate, emptiness filling him down to his core. Before he turned onto the street, he looked back. Flora had joined Theo and Callum on the step and she watched him, her hands clenched at her sides.

And since he hadn't earned that one, last, beautiful glimpse of her, he rode away, knowing that his life would never be the same. In more ways than one.

CHAPTER 14

Two days later, Flora sat in Valaria's parlor, staring straight ahead as the world moved around her. Her friends were all there, Callum and Valaria, Theo and Bernadette, bringing her tea that she let go cold, trying to offer her gentle support, talking about Roarke in angry terms. This was the first time she'd allowed that since she'd heard the truth. After he'd left her home, she had begged for privacy and taken to her bed like some gothic heroine. But there was only so much weeping one could do.

And only so much avoidance her friends would allow. So she was here now. Only she was still very much alone. She heard and felt none of their words and emotions. She heard and felt nothing at all, at present, except for pain when she let herself recall all the moments she'd shared with Roarke. He'd said they were real. But how could that be possible? That was the question.

Worse, if they were, then she had truly lost something that mattered.

"Dearest," Bernadette said, sitting beside her and touching her hand to bring her back to the room. "Please, isn't there something we can do?"

Valaria and Bernadette had already been told the truth by the gentlemen before they'd even stormed her house and found her with Roarke. At least she hadn't had to explain. And yet the fact that she had been the last to know about how foolish she'd been was another humiliation to add to the pile at her feet.

"No," she said softly. "I think this is one of those things that will just take time. I suppose I have an unending supply of it now since I have no interest in going back out or seeing anyone for a while."

Valaria came to set a hand on her shoulder from behind the settee. "As someone who has been trapped in the house for almost a year thanks to the requirements of mourning, I cannot recommend that, my dear, though I understand the sentiment. Perhaps we can find some other way to handle this."

"Such as?" Flora asked on a humorless laugh. "I certainly hope you don't expect me to go out and smile for everyone else's benefit."

"We could go to my estate in Blackvale," Callum said with a glance for Valaria. "It's only a day and half's ride—we could all go down together in a caravan."

Flora let out a low breath. "Run away."

Actually, that sounded like a fine idea. At present she was very interested in changing her name, fleeing to the Continent and becoming a recluse that her Italian neighbors might label an eccentric. Anything to avoid being seen by any other person. Anything to avoid ever catching an accidental glimpse of Roarke and having her world torn to shreds all over again.

"Not running away," Bernadette said gently. "Just a little escape where there are no eyes watching except for ours. Where you don't have to hide at all—you can just be."

Flora pondered the idea. On one hand, she didn't necessarily want to be alone with her thoughts out in the quiet countryside. When she was in her home, staring up at her ceiling, those thoughts were already very loud. But on the other hand, outside of London she wouldn't have to fear encountering her wicked stepchildren or Roarke.

And she could collect herself. She had to. After all, she'd known the man for only a few weeks. She couldn't let him affect her so. In the countryside, with the leaves changing beautifully and the company so kind and friendly, she could purposefully rebuild her walls and forget. She *needed* to forget him.

"It's a kind offer, Callum," she said, and then nodded. "Yes. I think that would be very nice. I'll make arrangements with my servants. When do you wish to leave?"

"Tomorrow," Callum said, and flashed a broad smile at Valaria. "I can make all our arrangements. I cannot wait for you to see the place!"

He sounded so thrilled and Valaria's eyes danced. Flora couldn't help but smile at this glimpse of their excitement, their love. Their future was off in the countryside, waiting for a matter of months to start. She was happy for them as they held hands, their eyes locked and their smiles impossible to temper.

Of course, she felt empty, too. Right now she couldn't imagine she'd ever feel anything like that again. Except she had, hadn't she? When she spent time with Roarke she'd felt some fluttering of those deeper emotions. A beckoning to a future that was now...gone.

She got up and paced to the window where she looked outside. "I look forward to the trip," she forced herself to say. "Now can we please change the subject? I don't want to be dour Flora, I don't want all your pitying looks and gentle words. If I am to go to the countryside to overcome my heartbr—" She cut herself off with a shake of her head. "No, not heartbreak. That gives something silly too much weight, doesn't it? Overcome my humiliation. If I'm to do that, let me start now. Will someone please share some gossip about someone's ugly dress or grasping elopement or anything to take my mind off a man I hardly knew?"

She still saw their pity as she turned toward them, but Theo forced a smile. "I have a little gossip to share."

And he began, talking about some meanspirited countess they all knew and how she'd gotten her comeuppance when she fell off her horse into the mud at Hyde Park in front of the Regent. It was a funny story and they all laughed. And Flora tried to ignore that she still felt disconnected. She could only hope her time in the country would cure her of this.

And she'd go back to normal somehow.

Roarke sat across from his mother at the small table, her plate pulled across to him. She smiled at him, a little uncertainly, as he carefully sliced up her food into manageable bites. Sometimes she could do this for herself, but confusion about the process was becoming more common.

"There," he said as he finished. "Much better, isn't it?"

She picked up her fork to eat. "You seem a nice gentleman," she said.

Roarke ignored the pain that throbbed through him at those words. She didn't know who he was at present. But she seemed to trust him and that was enough.

"Do I?" he asked as he finally took a bite of his own food. It tasted like sand, just like everything had tasted like sand since the moment Flora had found out the truth about him.

He pushed those thoughts aside to focus on his mother. She was nodding. "I think my boy would like you. And my husband."

Behind him, he heard Hilde take in a little breath as she bustled around doing a few chores while she wasn't distracted by Roarke's mother's needs. He managed not to react the same way.

"I'm sure I'd like your husband and your son," he said gently, and set the fork down. He wouldn't eat anything else today. He hadn't the heart now. "I hope I would live up to their expectations and yours."

She smiled. "If you're kind and honest, that's all you can be in this world."

He nodded. "You always said that, all my life. How I wish I could get your advice for what has happened."

"What has happened?" she asked.

He stared at her. She might not know him, but that didn't mean she didn't have something to add. He cleared his throat. Hilde had slipped from the room. He leaned a little closer to his mother.

"What if...what if someone *wasn't* kind and honest? Especially honest. What if they made a mistake, a brutal mistake? Did something wrong, even if they felt they had no choices. Even if it was to protect someone they loved? And then they hurt someone who didn't deserve it? How could they overcome that? How could *I* overcome that, Mama?"

"Who did you hurt, Roarke?" she asked.

He blinked. She'd called him by his name, and he caught her hands on the table and tried not to let the stinging tears in his eyes fall. "A lady," he said. "A beautiful woman named Flora."

"Everyone makes mistakes," his mother said. "All we can do is own them and try to do better. To show we are worthy of forgiveness through our deeds, even if we don't demand it. Build back trust, one person at a time, and be accepting if it is something permanently broken."

"Yes," he whispered. "I suppose that is true."

"We aren't just our mistakes," she said, and then drew her hands away. "And I'm sure you didn't mean to do something wrong. I may not know you, but you have kind eyes."

Roarke let out his breath and got to his feet. And she was gone again, forgetting him. He leaned down and kissed her forehead. "They're your eyes, Mama. And now I must go. I have a great deal to do. I'll send Hilde back in momentarily, yes? You eat in the meanwhile."

She did as she was told and didn't say goodbye. He stepped out of the little parlor and into the hall. Hilde was waiting.

"I know it's asking a great deal," he said. "But I did collect a small sum of money and I'll be finishing the improvements and increasing your wage within a few weeks. I hope you can be patient, even if I don't deserve further consideration."

Hilde looked past him into the room where his mother was quietly eating. She sighed. "You know I adore you dear mother. And I can see you're under a great deal of strain, Mr. Desmond. I'll keep on as I have been. But...I have responsibilities, too."

"I know." He shook his head. "I'm sorry. Thank you, Hilde."

She inclined her head and then moved past him into the parlor. "And how is the food, dear?"

"Who was that man, Hilde? He seemed sad."

Roarke flinched and strode from the house so he wouldn't hear or see more. He was about to swing up on his horse when a carriage pulled up onto the street and blocked his exit. He sighed as he saw the crest on the door. The Duke of Sidmouth. It seemed his cousin was here to collect.

Only when the door to the carriage opened, it wasn't Thomas who was leaning out, but Gertrude. She glanced at the little home he'd just exited, her mouth drawing down in a tight frown, and then said, "Get in."

He blinked at her. "What are you about, Gertrude? I'm not leaving my horse behind. Why are you here?"

"My footman will ride your mount so you may continue on your way after we talk." Gertrude speared him with a forceful look. "*Please*, Roarke. I need to speak to you privately. Now."

There was something in the desperation of her expression, in the white-knuckled grip she had on the edge of the carriage door. It might be merely dramatic effect that caused it—Gertrude had always been a bit dramatic—but he didn't want to risk that she actually had something meaningful to say.

Her footman was coming down from the back of the rig, and Roarke handed over the reins of the horse to him with a sigh before he climbed up into the carriage, settled into a place across from Gertrude and watched as she slammed the door and then banged on the wall behind her for her driver to move.

"Did you know that Flora went to the countryside with her friends?" Gertrude asked with no other preamble.

Roarke winced at the mention of Flora. He certainly didn't want to discuss her with her very tormenter. "No," he said through clenched teeth. "Though since you went to all the trouble to determine my location and demand I come into your carriage, I assume that means you three have realized that I failed in your vile objective. If you are here to threaten me, I already know you'll be preparing to destroy me."

Gertrude looked rather sick in that moment. "I'm certain my brothers will get to you. But right now they're focused on her. Time is running out. The clause in the inheritance will be activated in three weeks."

Roarke gripped his fists against his thighs and tried to meter his breath. There was no need to become protective—it wasn't his place. Not anymore. Flora was with her friends, Gertrude said, which likely meant Callum and Theo were part of that equation. He had already warned her about his cousins' intentions to hire anyone to seduce her, not just himself. There was nothing else that could be done, and Flora had asked him to leave her alone. If he was going to prove his true sorrow for his actions, he had to honor her request.

"If she is with her friends, I doubt they can reach her. Their idea to send some random man to seduce her underestimates her anyway," he said.

"I hate that woman," Gertrude said. "She stole my father's affection and attention. She replaced my mother and made him love her most. Made him forget his first wife." She shook her head. "But I'm...I'm afraid this isn't about seduction or ruination anymore, Roarke. I'm afraid they're going to have her killed."

Those words hit him as hard as a blast to the chest would have. He recoiled. "What?"

Gertrude's breath grew short. "You know that Philip has always been wild. Violent." The way she turned her head made Roarke wonder briefly if that violence had ever been turned on her. If that was part of why she encouraged it, to make him veer toward another victim.

"Thomas manages him," Roarke said softly, but he couldn't help but think of Philip arriving at his home the previous week. Making his threats.

"Thomas has thrown up his hands in disgust after your failure and wants no part in the resolution of the matter. He told Philip he didn't care how it was done. I think he thought there might be strong arming or intimidation…but Philip would do anything to impress our brother, *anything*. I overheard him in one of the parlors just yesterday with some wretched, vile criminal. He said he wanted her gone and it was evident *gone* didn't mean out of town."

"Did you talk to Thomas about it?" Roarke burst out.

"I tried," Gertrude said. "But he was going away to handle some estate business for a few days and he didn't want to hear it. He said I was hysterical."

"Fuck," Roarke muttered, and didn't care that he'd cursed in front of his maiden cousin. "Let me out."

Gertrude blinked. "What, but I wanted to talk more about—"

He leaned over her and banged on the wall behind her. "No, let me out."

"Why?"

"Do you know where they were going?" he asked. "A friend in the country. Was it the Duke of Blackvale or the Duke of Lightmorrow?"

She stared. "How did you know?"

"Because I know her. And I know her friends." He gulped back his fear. "Tell me which one."

"Blackvale," she said softly. "They left two days ago."

The carriage stopped and Roarke jumped down even as it still rocked. He leaned back in and speared his cousin with a glare. "You said this happened yesterday. Did you send a message to Flora, telling her she might be in danger?"

Gertrude shifted and the fear flashed in her eyes again. "N-No," she admitted. "I thought my brothers might find out and then it would be me who was threatened. I thought…I thought…"

"We're all cowards in this family," Roarke said. "And I can only hope that our spectacular failures as human beings won't lead to harm to a woman who deserves nothing but the best things in this world. Deserves better than us, for certain."

With that he slammed the carriage door in her face, grabbed the reins of his horse from the confused servant who had been riding him but jumped down when he saw Roarke get out of the carriage, and rode off at full speed to exit London.

He had to get to Flora. Nothing else mattered. He could only hope that it wouldn't be too late.

CHAPTER 15

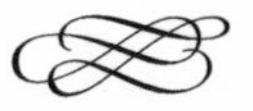

If Flora had hoped that going to a new location would quell the pain in her heart, she determined within a day of her arrival to Callum's estate that it wasn't meant to be. Now instead of sitting on her own veranda, staring out at fluttering leaves and trying not to cry, she looked over Callum's foggy, moody estate grounds instead.

At least it was a change in scenery. But she couldn't seem to change her heart. Why did this hurt so much? Why couldn't she just write Roarke off and come back to herself? She feared the answer that sometimes woke her at night. Feared emotions that, if she accepted them, would only make all this worse.

"You look cold."

She jolted at the voice close to her and looked up to see Bernadette had joined her on the terrace. She held out Flora's spencer and she got to her feet as she took it.

"I didn't even notice the chill," Flora admitted even though now the breeze cut through her a bit more. "Thank you."

Bernadette helped her slip the short jacket over her arms and Flora buttoned it while she continued to look out into the distance. She was warm now, but still empty.

"I know I must try to be a better companion during this trip," she said with a sigh.

"Don't be silly—you are a lovely companion," Bernadette said, giving Flora's waist a little squeeze.

"Well, then I must find some way to shake off these doldrums if only for myself."

"I know you're suffering."

Flora rolled her eyes. "But why? I knew Roarke Desmond for a few weeks. I shared a handful of kisses and one...well, *encounter* on my settee." She shivered as she remembered his mouth on her, her body convulsing with pleasure. "I should not be so forlorn like he was a lover for years with promises made and expectations created."

"Expectations can be created in a night," Bernadette said with a slight tremor to her voice. "I watched you with the man, I listened to you talk about him. Perhaps the acquaintance was brief, but it meant something to you. Trying to pretend it didn't won't help you get over your disappointment. Whatever his motives, yours were pure. Your emotions were real. I hate to see you try to discount them as a way to stop hurting. I can tell you from bitter experience that it doesn't work."

Flora bent her head. "Perhaps you're right. But if I admit that I... I cared for him, oh even saying the words stings."

"Understandably," Bernadette said. "Because he lied and broke your trust and made you question yourself."

"I think what's worse is that I believe what he told me when I confronted him. I believe that he did truly care about me. That much of what we shared was real, despite his ulterior motives. That the connection we were forming could have been—" Flora broke off.

Bernadette took her hand. "If you have to mourn a future, it's fine."

"Hmmm." Flora stared off into the distance. The woods beyond the main estate grounds were as tangled and cold as her heart at present. "Perhaps I'll take a walk. I know it's to rain the next few days, so this will be the last time I can stretch my legs and hopefully clear my mind."

"A capital idea," Bernadette agreed. "I'll go with you."

Flora turned toward her friend, saw the lingering pity in her stare. Hated it, even as she adored Bernadette for wishing to take care of her.

She gripped Bernadette's hand and said, "No, dearest. While I appreciate the constant care you and the others have shown to me since we left London, I think the best thing I can do is go for a walk alone and have a stern talk to myself. And I promise when I come back I will laugh and play games and exchange knowing glances with you about Callum and Valaria."

Bernadette smiled. "If you think it will help, I would never stop you. But do be careful."

"I will," Flora promised, and gave her hand a last squeeze before she walked across the large veranda to a short flight of stone steps that led down to the garden below.

She felt Bernadette watching her as she moved through perfectly trimmed, now leafless hedgerows and past covered beds of flowers, ready for their winter slumber. She had revealed too much to her friend...and to herself in their conversation. Now she had to sit with feelings she had been afraid to name.

She had cared for Roarke. And she'd known that feeling could develop into something much more powerful. Much more lasting. She'd known she could love him.

She stumbled a little with that thought. Love him. Let him love her. And she could picture it all in a rush of laughter and art and long conversations about current events. She could picture him pleasing her, touching her, taking her like she'd so desperately wanted him to do on the settee that day. She could picture a little life together. Not desperately exciting, but content and filled with passion.

That was what she'd lost when she realized he'd come to her from a lie. And it hurt. It hurt so much that she wanted to run from it.

There was a low gate in the distance, and beyond it, the wooded peace of the untamed part of Callum's estate. There was a trail through the brambles and she followed it, stepping over dead sticks and crunching through the fallen leaves. There was a smell of smoke to the air—perhaps someone was burning leaves in another part of the property—but it left a crisp bite that made her breathe a little deeper. Yes, this was what she needed. This type of peace alone here in the woods that helped her shove those painful thoughts aside and not continue to have them torment her.

Except just as that thought calmed her, she noticed there was a man ahead of her on the trail. He was very tall, very broad shouldered, and as she stopped in the middle of the path, she could see he had a hard, cruel expression on his face. He spat off the side of the trail and then smiled at her, though it was not a pleasant expression. Her heart began to pound.

"What are you doing out here, little mouse?" he asked.

She took a step back, and he moved forward the equal distance. "I was walking through the estate of my *friend*, the Duke of Blackvale. This is his land, sir. I believe you might be trespassing. You'll have to ask him when he and his party joins me in a few moments."

She lied, of course. But she hoped she sounded truthful, so this man wouldn't know she was all alone, without anyone from back in the house likely to hear her if she cried out. She hadn't gone all that far off the main part of the grounds, but far enough that her voice might not carry and no one would notice her missing for a while.

"Now, now, lying ain't very ladylike," he drawled, and now he stepped toward her again. He had a big scar across his eye, like a knife had slashed him at some point. It only added to the terrifying presence of the man.

"I-I'm not lying," she stammered.

"'Course you are. I *know* you're by yourself. This ain't personal, you know." He moved closer again and now he withdrew a long blade from a sheath at his hip. "Though I won't say I won't enjoy what happens first."

She staggered back, ready to pivot and run, but she tripped over a rock on the trail, stumbling onto her backside. He darted forward and she braced, ready to feel his weight come down on her, his knife through her. But it didn't. Before he could crash down over her and do whatever horrible things he had planned, the figure of a man flew from the woods and hit her attacker, flinging both men off the path and into the tangled woods.

Flora rolled to her knees and her breath caught. It was no stranger who had interrupted this attack. It was Roarke! And now he and the scarred man were struggling over the villain's knife.

"No!" she screamed, and got to her feet. She should have run, of course, but she didn't want to leave Roarke. Her attacker was bigger than him and now he looked enraged, like a bull in a paddock. She started to scream, "Help! Help!" over and over.

Her attacker looked up at her, clearly annoyed, and that seemed to give Roarke a chance. He tugged the knife free and stabbed it into the attacker's shoulder. The man howled in pain and began to curse as he pulled the knife from his body, and then swung the handle across Roarke's forehead. The wooden handle cut open a gash across Roarke's eyebrow and he fell off the attacker with a grunt.

The man glanced toward the big house, looked at Flora and smiled. "See you soon, Your Grace!" Then he bounded off into the woods.

Flora hurled herself forward, off the path to where Roarke lay. He was awake, but his gaze was unsteady as he struggled to sit up. Blood poured down his face from where his forehead had split open, dripping from his chin.

"Roarke," she whispered, reaching up to press her hand against the cut on his forehead. "Oh God."

"You have to go," Roarke murmured. "He might come back."

"I'm not leaving you," she said. She looked back over her shoulder at the house. A servant was running toward them, likely drawn by her screams. Perhaps the attacker had seen the man and that was part of why he'd run off. "Hurry!" she cried out.

The young man reached them and his eyes went wide. "Your Grace!"

"Mr. Desmond and I were attacked," she explained without preamble. "Hurry, fetch the duke and his party! And tell them to call for a doctor."

The young man gasped and then stammered, "Y-Yes! Right away!"

He took off running back up the path at full speed.

"Go with him," Roarke insisted, and tried to get up. He staggered and went back down to his knees.

"No," she insisted. "Please just wait here, Roarke. Let them come help you, you're hurt."

"I don't want you out here where that monster could return for you," Roarke insisted, and clung to her arm. Together they managed to get him up. He wobbled, but she buoyed him up as they slowly moved toward the house. It felt like a snail's pace and she could see him wobbling in and out of reality as they moved. She had to keep him with her because if he fell she'd never get him back up.

"Roarke," she said.

"Hm?"

"Stay with me now. Why in the world were you here?" she asked, trying to hold him up with one hand and press the other to his gushing head wound.

He grunted. "My cousins," he gasped. His voice broke a little. "I… I heard they were sending someone here to…to hurt you."

Flora's ears began to ring at those words. Her stepchildren had created this situation? They hated her so much that they would hire someone to hurt her? Kill her? Her stomach turned and she fought not to cast up her accounts.

Roarke was still talking. "So I…I followed you…found him… stopped him."

He said nothing more because at that point there was shouting from up the path. Relief filled Flora as Callum and Theo came into view, running at full speed toward her, calling out for them.

"What the bloody hell?" Callum said as he stared at Roarke.

"We were attacked!" Flora called out as the two dukes reached them. "Roarke saved me."

He staggered then, and Theo jumped forward and caught him. Together he and Callum gripped Roarke beneath each arm and moved him up the trail. It was only when she no longer had to physically support him that Flora began to shake. Even when they reached the gate back into the safety of the garden, she couldn't stop trembling.

Servants were gathering, flowing from the house, running around, looking for direction. Callum began shouting orders, calling for a room to be readied, insuring someone had gone for the doctor.

She hardly heard any of it now that she didn't have to be in charge of taking care of Roarke. All she could do was follow, staring at his blood on her hands, thinking about what would have happened if he hadn't come. What *had* happened when he did. And why he'd said she'd been attacked.

Her stepchildren. They were so bound by their hate and greed that they wouldn't stop at humiliation and heartbreak. They wanted physical pain. They wanted death even, because that was what Flora had seen in that man's eyes when he moved on her. He was going to kill her.

And only Roarke had prevented that inevitability.

They entered the house and Bernadette and Valaria came running into the foyer. Their horror at seeing the blood on Roarke's face was clear. He continued to wobble and then he started to slide to the floor.

He looked toward Flora, his eyes wide, and he said, "Please, protect my mother."

Then his head lolled back and he lost consciousness.

CHAPTER 16

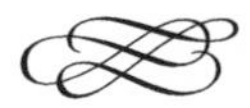

"What happened?"

Flora blinked as Valaria asked the question but didn't look away from the door in front of her. Behind it was a chamber where the dukes and a few servants had carried Roarke what felt like a lifetime ago. No one had exited since, though the doctor had been brought in when he arrived a few moments before.

And through it all, Flora had stayed there, staring, praying that someone would come out, would tell her that Roarke was well. She didn't know much, but she couldn't believe that losing that much blood was a good thing.

"Flora." Valaria's tone was gentler. "Please."

"Why don't we come away, dearest?" Bernadette said. "Theo said it would be a little while when the doctor arrived. We can clean you up."

"I don't need to clean up," Flora whispered.

"You're covered in blood, sweet," Valaria said.

Flora blinked and looked down at herself. She'd known her hands were bloody, but now she saw there was also blood on her gown. And grass and mud stains. Because she'd been attacked. Because Roarke had been injured.

She wobbled a little and Valaria caught her, shoring her up. "Come," she ordered, and drew Flora up the hall just a few doors to the chamber Valaria had been sharing with Callum. "We won't go far. And I'll tell a servant to let us know as soon as the doctor has finished."

Flora let them take her. She sat where she was directed to sit in the chamber and watched as Valaria rushed back out to tell the servants what to do. There was a basin of clean water by the window and Bernadette got a cloth. She returned to sit across from Flora and slowly began to wipe her hands clean.

But even as the blood was washed away, Flora feared she would never be the same. Because of what had happened to her and because it had been Roarke who rode to her rescue.

"I know you must be afraid," Bernadette said, squeezing her hands before she returned to the basin and rinsed the cloth, turning the water pink.

Flora turned her head. "He came out of nowhere," she whispered.

"The man who attacked?"

She nodded and then wrinkled her brow. "And Roarke. He came out of nowhere and he...he saved me." She bent her head. "What if he dies? What if I lose him?"

Bernadette returned to her side and held her gently for a moment before she went back to washing away the blood on her skin. "He won't die."

"How can you know that?" she sobbed softly.

Bernadette tilted her chin up. "Because it seems he might have too much to live for."

Flora sucked in a breath and then leaned forward to rest her forehead on Bernadette's shoulder. She had no idea if that was true, or if her hopes and fears and will could somehow keep Roarke safe.

All she knew was that she couldn't imagine losing him for good. She couldn't imagine anything but being able to go into that room and find him whole and well for her. So she kept hoping, praying as the clock ticked mercilessly in the background.

Roarke's head was swimming, though he was beginning to have more clarity as he sat on the bed in a fine chamber in Callum's home, the doctor perched beside him, stitching the gash above his eyebrow.

He winced as the needle pierced his flesh and looked to where Callum and Theo were standing, both watching him with unreadable expressions. "I'm sorry," he said when the silence felt like it stretched for a lifetime. "For what I did in London. I'm sorry."

Callum turned away and Theo drew in a long breath. "It's her you need to apologize to, not us. Though I suppose saving her life goes a long way toward that."

Roarke gripped his hands at his sides. "I do owe you an apology regardless. Callum, you accused me of using our friendship to get to her, and you were right. I did."

Callum cursed beneath his breath and shook his head, his disdain for Roarke written all over his face. After the weeks of renewed friendship, it stung to see it here. Stung worse that he entirely deserved it.

"It was bloody awful," he continued. "I hated myself for it. And if you two hate me for the rest of my life, as well, I will have earned that ire. As for her...I didn't come here because I wanted to earn back her regard. I came here because I knew my cousins were determined to harm her."

"Your cousins were behind this?" Theo burst out as both men moved toward him.

The doctor placed a hand against Roarke's throbbing forehead. "Hold still now. You're going to make it worse."

"Hardly possible," Roarke said. "And yes. The man who attacked her and did this to me was hired by my cousins. It seems that if they cannot ruin her, at least one of them believes the answer is to end her."

His blood ran cold with that thought. And with the memory of what he had seen that day. "I came here to warn her and found out that there was a man asking about her at the inn. I managed to follow him and that's how I was able to stop him when he attacked her."

She had been on her back on the trail, her hands raised, her eyes filled with fear as that bastard loomed over her, knife in his hand and cruel intentions in his eyes. Roarke would have done anything to save her in that moment. He would have sacrificed everything and anything. And perhaps he had.

"Are you almost finished?" he asked the doctor. "I must ride back to London."

The doctor lifted his eyes with a snort. "You aren't riding a horse after you lost consciousness from a blow to the head. You need to stay quiet for at least a day or two to recover."

"I cannot," Roarke said, and started to shove past the man to get up off the bed. The doctor pushed him back and Callum stepped forward to do the same.

"You must listen to him now," Callum said. "You'll kill yourself."

"That man is not going to stop," Roarke said, even as his knees wobbled. "And while he would be a fool to try to strike against Flora here while she's under your protection, I'm certain he'll go back to my cousins and report what happened. Their ire will turn toward me, and the best way to hurt me is to…to harm my mother."

Theo let out a breath. "You said something about that to Flora in the foyer. How could they harm her?"

"She…she is not capable of taking care of herself. Her mind is going." His eyes burned with tears of grief and terror. "And I have very little to maintain her. She lives all but alone, just a companion to assist her. She cannot be left so unprotected now that I know how far my cousins are willing to go. I must go back. I must find some other place to take her…"

He rested back with a moan of both physical and emotional pain. Where? Where could he take her? His little hovel was barely fit for himself. He couldn't afford to let another arrangement and there would be no money coming from his cousins ever again, he was certain. If they were serious about destroying him, she would burn, too.

"I'll go back to London," Theo said gently. "Look at me."

Roarke blinked to clear his vision and did so. Theo was looking at him evenly, all sparkling humor gone from his eyes. "I will go back to London today, ride as hard and fast as I can," he said. "I will look into ways to prove that your cousins were involved in this attack that could be used against them. Additionally, I will immediately move your mother and her companion to a safe place. My own home, if need be."

"She won't understand," Roarke said, sitting up again. "She'll be confused."

"And I will be kind and gentle and make sure she is a little disrupted as I can make her." Theo started across the room. "I'll go get ready to depart and you write a letter explaining my presence to your mother's companion so she won't be resistant to my help."

"Theo," Roarke called, stopping him at the door. He turned back and Roarke shook his head. "I cannot repay you."

"Make it up to *her*," Theo said. "You've made yourself square with me."

He left then, and Roarke caught his breath. He hadn't expected forgiveness from any of these people, and yet Theo offered not just that, but help beyond his wildest imagining. The idea that his mother would be unreachable was an enormous relief.

He looked at Callum. "I know you don't feel the same."

Callum pursed his lips. "No. But you may make it up to me yet. I'm sure Flora and the other ladies are awaiting news of you. I'll go tell them you are going to survive. And try to explain to my future bride, who is not so very forgiving, that you will be our houseguest for a few days while you recover."

He left then and the doctor began to put away his materials and talk to Roarke about what he needed to do for his wound and for the blow to the head that had caused it. But Roarke wasn't listening. All he could think about was Flora. And that he would be forced into her proximity all over again, only this time without lies between them.

Whether she would allow him to be close to her or make what he had done up to her was another question entirely.

Flora had further explained what had happened in the woods while Bernadette and Valaria helped her clean up and change into a different gown from the one now stained with Roarke's blood. Their looks of horror had brought back her own feelings of terror, grief…and relief when Roarke appeared, her savior from the dark.

"I want to go back to the hallway and wait for the doctor to come out," Flora said, her voice trembling. "I need to know that Roarke is going to recover."

Valaria let out a long breath. "Yes, of course. But before we return, I want to ask you something and I need you to really think about the answer."

Flora forced herself to focus on her friend and frowned. Valaria looked very serious now. Grim. "I don't like your expression."

"Yes, this man came careening out of the woods and saved you. But do…do you think he created this scenario as a way to get close to you?" Valaria asked.

Bernadette gasped. "Valaria!"

"I hate to think of it too," Valaria said with a quick glance at their friend. "But Roarke already lied—we can't assume he wouldn't do worse."

Flora knew why Valaria would think that, but hearing those words made her own feelings on the subject starkly clear.

"Yes, we can," Flora said, firm and filled with faith. "A liar is not the same as this. I have no doubt that Roarke wasn't involved in *any* way in the attack. I know him...even with the lies, I know him well enough to know that. Even if I didn't, he was too brutal in the way he hit the man, stabbed him in the shoulder, and he was badly hurt."

Her voice faded as she thought of Roarke dripping in his own blood, his gaze unsteady from the strike that monster who attacked her had thrown. "I've never seen so much blood." She dropped her head and felt the tears start to fall, her terror returning immediately as she asked the question she had kept asking over and over, "Do you think he'll live?"

"Head wounds bleed, even when they're not serious," Valaria said gently, for what had to be the third time. "And Callum seems certain his doctor is the best in the area. I think he'll be fine. But it's evident that you still care about this man, that he means more to you than beyond that he protected you."

Flora gripped her hands at her side. "Yes," she whispered. "I know you think I'm a fool."

Valaria's expression softened. "No, my dear, not you. You are not a fool for caring. He is a fool for not being a better steward of your heart when he was so lucky as to earn even a part of it." She took her hand. "But I am very grateful to him for saving you."

"Can we go to him then? And wait?" Flora asked.

Valaria nodded, and together the three of them left the chamber and moved back into the hallway to wait. Callum was already there, and he straightened from his position leaning against the wall when they stepped into view. Valaria rushed to him, leaned up to kiss his cheek. Their eyes met and a world of communication flowed through them.

"Is he well?" Flora asked, and her voice broke. "Is he safe?"

Callum stepped away from Valaria and took both of Flora's hands. His dark eyes locked with hers and his calm made her feel some fraction of the same. "He is fine," he said. "He'll have a nasty scar as a reminder and his head isn't entirely clear, but I assure you, he will survive. The doctor just departed and Theo is inside, finishing up some conversation before he leaves for London."

Bernadette stepped forward. "Theo is leaving?" she asked.

Callum glanced at her. "Yes," he said. "He is going back to do some investigating of the attacker and also to help set up protections for Roarke's mother. I know he wants to see you before he goes."

Bernadette nodded, her breath a little short, and Flora almost sagged with relief. "I'm glad he'll help her. Roarke was so fearful for her safety. And that will allow him to recover." She looked at the door. "I want to see him. I don't want to wait."

Callum hesitated and exchanged another quick look with Valaria, but then motioned his hand. "I'm sure he and Theo won't mind the interruption."

She was already moving to open and step through the door. She found Roarke on the bed. His forehead was bandaged, the blood had been cleaned up by the doctor so there were no remnants now. He was shirtless and barefoot, lying on top of the coverlet, propped up on the pillows, talking to Theo.

Neither man had noticed her entry, so she got to hear the end of their exchange.

"I know I don't deserve your help. But I deeply appreciate it, Theo," Roarke said as he handed over a letter. "Hilde should agree to assist you in making my mother comfortable with these instructions."

Theo took the letter and nodded. "I'll do everything in my power to help make this right on all accounts. I know you'll do the same." He turned and saw her, and Roarke followed his gaze.

He caught his breath and Flora did the same. Theo gave a thin smile. "I'll leave you two and get on my way. I'll write as soon as I can and update you," he said.

As he left, Theo squeezed her arm and then shut the door behind himself, leaving her alone with Roarke for the first time since his horrible secrets had been revealed. She moved toward him, almost not of her own will and stopped beside the bed.

"Roarke," she breathed as she reached out to gently touch the bandage on his head and then slid her fingers to his cheek. He leaned into her hand, his green gaze holding hers with more intensity than any man had ever looked at her in her entire life.

"You saved me," she whispered.

He shook his head and winced with the action. "Don't make me out to be a hero, Flora. I don't expect any quarter after what I've done."

She sat on the edge of the bed, so close to him, so very aware now that he was half-naked and extremely nicely made. She had the strangest desire to trace the muscles of his chest and stomach with her fingertip, but held back.

Instead she drew in a deep breath and whispered, "I'd like an explanation of how exactly you came to be here, Roarke. Please. I need the truth."

CHAPTER 17

After his lies had come out in such a terrible way, after he'd watched Flora's face crumple with betrayal and heartbreak, Roarke had fought to accept that he would never feel her touch again. He'd dreamed of it, of course, every night since they'd been parted. Sometimes he swore he could feel the weight of it, like the ghost of what he'd lost had passed by him.

But right now Flora was seated on the edge of the bed and she was still touching him. Her hand covered his, her fingers soft against his skin. And nothing else in the world mattered in that charged moment.

Except, of course, for the explanation he was about to give.

He told her everything. He told her about his cousins' continued threats, about Gertrude's arrival at his mother's, about his rush of a trip from London that was a blur. He spared no detail, even when he saw her flinch with pain and fear.

When he was finished, she stared at their intertwined fingers, silent. Pained. He could see that clearly. Fearful, but of course she would be.

"Thank you," she whispered, and looked up at him through her long lashes. "That was difficult to hear, but I appreciate knowing it all."

"If I can give you nothing else, I vow I will always give you the truth from this point forward," he said. "It won't make up for the lies before, but I owe you that, Flora. And so much more."

Her fingers tightened against his and she let out a shuddering breath. "Theo will do everything in his power to protect your mother."

"Yes," Roarke said, and relief flooded him. "And I believe he'll get to her first. I injured that villain as much or more than he injured me. I'm guessing it will take him a few days to limp back to Philip and report his failure. I doubt any moves will be made against my mother until then. So I can be relieved, and even more so when I hear from Theo that he has arrived and moved her to a safer place."

She leaned closer and now he could smell that sweetness to her skin. It reminded him of how she tasted when he kissed her lips. When he kissed other places.

"Thank you," she murmured. "Coming here has made your life more difficult, I know. That you did it means a great deal."

"I don't deserve to tell you why," he whispered. "Though I think you know why. I hurt you, Flora. And I never want to do that again, I never want to aid or abet someone else doing the same."

"I know," she said, her voice shaking.

She slid her hand up his bare arm, across his shoulder. They both watched it move together and he shivered at the warmth of her touch. He was trying to control himself, trying not to take something he didn't deserve. But she was making that very difficult.

She cupped his cheek again at last, her fingers splaying against his skin. She leaned in, her breath stirring his lips. When she kissed him, he couldn't hold back any longer. He gripped his hands against the coverlet so he wouldn't become too swept away, but he opened to her instantly.

And she took. Her tongue touched his, her lips became more seeking and she let out a soft moan that seemed to crack the world open before him. He drowned in her, tilting his head to deepen the kiss. It throbbed when he did so, but he didn't care about the pain, not when he was tangling with her tongue the same way he wanted to tangle with her body.

At last, he couldn't help himself. He cupped her neck with one hand, drawing her even closer until it was almost impossible to feel anything but her. Everything was her and he never wanted that to change.

But she stopped it at last. Not with haste, not with regret. She just drew back, her face still close to his, her hand curled around his arm while the other balanced against his bare chest. Her breath was short.

"I'm...still angry with you," she whispered.

He nodded slowly. "You deserve to be."

"And I don't know where to go from here."

He swallowed hard. "I'll go wherever you want to go, Flora. If I can make up to you even a fraction of the damage I did, I will move the world to do it. And if you kiss me now and never want to look at me again, I'll have to accept that even if it breaks my heart."

Her expression softened, but she stood up at last and took a step back to create more distance between them. "I know you must rest in the next few days and there will be a great deal to discuss when it comes to my future and how to manage the escalating situation with my stepchildren. But I...I also know we'll spend a great deal of time together. So I suppose we'll just have to see what happens."

"Yes," he said, and somehow masked the swell of hope those words she said gave him. And flattened by the realization that followed: he was in love with this woman.

She stepped to the door and opened it. "I...I hope..."

She shook her head and said nothing more, but slipped out, leaving him alone with a throbbing head and a sliver of the possibility that perhaps the future he'd thought he'd destroyed could be rebuilt.

Hours later, as Flora stood in the parlor with Bernadette, Valaria and Callum, she couldn't stop looking at the door. Waiting for Roarke. Thinking about the kiss they'd shared in the bedroom a few hours before. It was strange. She'd kissed him in London, done more than kiss him, but this almost felt like the first time.

Perhaps because there were no longer lies between them.

She shifted her weight and then looked at Valaria. Her friend was standing with Callum, but she was watching Flora right back. Flora huffed out a breath. "Are you going to invite him to join us for supper?

Valaria didn't ask her to clarify the *him*. She folded her arms. "He's resting."

Callum barked out a short laugh at his fiancée's response and then briefly rested a hand on her lower back, a show of support that Flora wished she could have so easily. Then he moved forward, his attention shifting to Flora. "I think you want to forgive him," he said gently.

And there it was, said out loud at last. She felt like a thousand candles were shining on her now and she was utterly revealed. She glanced first at Bernadette and then Valaria. Both her friends looked concerned, but there was no surprise to their expressions.

"I…don't know," she murmured. "He misrepresented himself and hurt my feelings. But I look at him and I…" She broke off and shook her head. "You all must think me the worst kind of pathetic fool."

To her surprise, it was Valaria who stepped forward, her expression much softer now. She wrapped her arms around Flora and hugged her. "Not at all. I know I've been…harsh about this. It's only that I worry about you. I was with a man who hurt me, and I want to protect you from ever feeling pain."

Flora squeezed her back and then stepped away. She held Valaria's gaze. "I love you for that. But you can't protect me from feeling pain. Just as I couldn't protect you when you were finding your way with Callum. Sometimes the way out is through, as much as we would try to stop those we care about from suffering."

Valaria blinked and Bernadette caught her breath. Even Callum seemed taken aback by that statement.

"I know you're right," Valaria said. "And I'll be more mindful of that. But I have to ask…do you think Roarke could mean as much to you as Callum means to me? Is that how deeply you feel for this man?"

Flora glanced at Callum, always at Valaria's side, her protector and friend and lover and future. And she could picture Roarke in the same position for herself. If they could overcome what had happened at the start, she believed in the deepest core of herself, that they could be happy in the future.

"Perhaps," she said slowly.

Valaria blanched, but then she straightened up and smoothed her skirts. "Then of course we will invite him to join us if he's up for it. I can ring for—"

"No, I'll go to him," Callum said. "I'll take care of it."

He gave Flora a soft smile before he slipped from the room. Her heart immediately began to pound as she watched him go, knowing that she had perhaps just begun a new chapter in the book of her life. And she hoped it would end well.

Roarke lay on the bed, staring up at the ceiling. He ought to have been sleeping, he supposed, recovering from his injuries. God knew he felt them. His head still ached dully and the stitches on his gash itched. But it wasn't those things that kept him from sleep.

No, it was thoughts of Flora. Her worry about his well-being, the way her hands flowed over his skin…her kiss. All he could think about was her kiss and what it meant. She said she was still angry—

she deserved to be angry. But she still kissed him and his hope still soared.

There was a light knock on his door and he straightened a fraction, his heart leaping a the possibility that it could be her. "Come in," he called out.

When the door opened, it wasn't Flora. Callum stepped in and then leaned on the doorjamb, arms crossed over his chest. "You look a little better. Although those bruises are fairly horrific."

Roarke reached up to touch his own face and winced. The way his eye felt, he was certain the bruising had extended lower than the bandage covering. Wonderful.

He forced a laugh. "If it helps, I also feel like shit."

"Too shit to come to dinner?" Callum asked. "Because you're invited."

"By you?" Roarke asked, wincing when he lifted his eyebrows.

Callum shook his head slowly. "No. By *Flora*."

Roarke caught his breath at the revelation, but then he shut his eyes. "I came here with nothing but my horse and the clothes on my back. Not fit for a supper gathering even if they weren't covered in blood and dirt and likely being cleaned by your poor staff at present."

Callum shrugged. "You can use some of my clothing. It might be a bit ill-fitting, but I doubt anyone will care, least of all Flora. And my valet can help you dress. If, that is, you actually want to try."

Roarke stared at him. Callum wasn't talking about trying to get dressed or trying to join the party, that was clear. He was talking about trying with Flora. Trying for a future he didn't deserve and couldn't see a path to, even though he desperately wanted it and her.

And yet he couldn't refuse the chance. Couldn't turn away from the possibility.

"Of course I'll try," he said, pushing the covers away from his legs and gingerly coming down from the high bed. He gripped the edge as he tested his knees. Unlike earlier in the day, they no longer felt like jelly, so that was an improvement.

"Wonderful. My valet, Bledsoe, will be up shortly with a few things for you to wear." Callum pivoted to go and then froze and turned back. "I wasn't going to do this, but I think I must. Are you in love with her?"

Roarke lifted his gaze to his friend and clung to the edge of the bed even tighter because the question weakened his knees now, instead of his injury. He straightened his shoulders and then nodded. "Yes."

Callum's eyes widened, but Roarke didn't let him respond. He continued, "But I've no expectations. I will make no demands."

Callum stepped into the chamber and shut the door behind him. He ran one hand through his hair and then he said, "My road with Valaria wasn't easy. I understand the desperation of perhaps never getting what you desire most. You do have a great deal to prove. If you want help, I'm here."

"Why?" Roarke burst out without thinking, and then shook his head. "I ask because I'm surprised to hear you say that after everything that transpired."

Callum let out his breath slowly. "I can see you were between a rock and a hard place when it came to this situation. And you made mistakes. However, I think a man is defined more by how he responds to his mistakes, isn't he? And I see how she lights up when she speaks about you. Perhaps you *both* deserve a second chance."

The idea that Flora still lit up when he was a topic warmed Roarke to his toes and the longing that had flared when she kissed him burned a little brighter.

"I'll send the valet and then go tell the ladies that you'll join us shortly."

"Thank you," Roarke said softly as Callum left with a wave of his hand.

He moved to the mirror above the fireplace and winced as he saw his bruised face. Saw his own hesitations and fears reflected in his eyes. But no, he had to be resolute not uncertain, because this was likely his only chance. He had to make the most of it.

CHAPTER 18

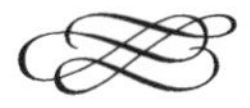

Flora was pacing the parlor, no longer capable of containing her nervousness as she awaited Roarke's arrival. And then...he was there. He strode through the door and she pivoted, her breath gone as she looked at him in his fine clothes. They were Callum's, but the lack of perfect fit didn't matter one bit to her. She was still bowled over by how handsome he was.

And by how damaged. Although his head was still wrapped in the linen bandage, the bruising from the blow crept below the stark white. It was black and blue along his eyebrow and down the side and bottom of his left eye.

"Oh, Roarke," she said as she moved toward him without a care to what the others saw when she did. She caught his hand. "Does it hurt terribly?"

He gave a half-smile that told the story before he said, "I might normally lie and tell you no, but I won't ever lie to you again. So yes, it hurts. But it's manageable."

She sucked in a breath at that casual promise never to lie again. It hung between them, heavy and sweet and she found herself praying it could be true.

"You really did almost die protecting her," Bernadette breathed as she stepped a little closer, staring at his injuries. "Thank you, Mr. Desmond."

Valaria moved forward now and gave him the slightest of smiles. But Flora knew how much that meant. "We should go in for supper and Mr. Desmond can sit and rest."

She took Callum's arm and the couple led them through the door to the adjoining dining room. Bernadette smiled at Flora and then followed, leaving her alone, albeit briefly, with Roarke.

"May I take you?" he asked.

Once again her breath caught. She knew he was talking about escorting her into supper, but those weren't the images her errant mind created. She was breathless as she said, "Yes. Please. Certainly. Yes."

He chuckled a little at her flustered response, but then held out his elbow and together they stepped into the next room. Valaria had indicated Flora and Roarke be seated next to each other, with Roarke between her and Callum at the head of the table, Valaria across from him and Bernadette on her other side. Flora almost laughed at the absurdity that Roarke was now surrounded by her friends. But if he felt the circle tightening around him, he said nothing and simply helped her to her place and settled, slowly, into his own.

Supper began, dishes were brought, and to Flora's relief, the night didn't turn into an interrogation of Roarke. They talked of normal subjects: plays and books, the roads and the state of the government. It was as if her friends had decided to accept this man she cared for back into their circle for a while. And while she knew they were judging him, watching him, they weren't trying to catch him in some trap.

It was Bernadette who broached the first difficult subject, as dessert was brought out and placed before them: a small selection of biscuits with sweet wine to dip them into. "I'm sorry to hear about your mother's condition, Mr. Desmond."

Flora watched Roarke's response. His mouth tightened and he

set a biscuit back on the small plate before him. He looked up at Bernadette. "Thank you, Your Grace."

Everyone had reverted back to formality, which Flora knew was to be expected, but she missed the easiness between them, especially with this subject.

"How long has she been ill?" Bernadette pressed.

"A few years, though her confusion has progressed a great deal in the last six months," he said.

Flora could feel him forcing himself to be open, to give vulnerability rather than turtle up and protect himself. For her? Was it possible this was all part of his promise of honesty? She couldn't help but reach out and cover his hand with hers.

"That must be difficult," she said softly.

He nodded. "Yes. I hate to see her in this state. I hate knowing that I'm at a disadvantage in how to help her. It's not an excuse for the mistakes I've made, but it is partly my reason." His gaze went distant. "I hope that Theo...Lightmorrow...will be able to help her. That she'll respond well and not with fear because he's a stranger."

"He will," Bernadette said. "He has a vast capacity for kindness, gentleness, despite his reputation. And before he left, we talked together about strategies for how to approach her. I assure you he will be as soothing as you might wish."

Flora tilted her head because Bernadette's emotions were as plain in that moment as she feared her own must be. Her feelings for Theo were slashed across her face, though she schooled them immediately.

"I appreciate that, Your Grace," Roarke said. "It takes a great deal of weight from my shoulders knowing that he will be. And that you are part of that. Thank you."

Bernadette looked at him a long moment and then said, "I thought we agreed that you would call me Bernadette, Roarke."

Flora could have sobbed at that renewed acceptance and understanding from her sweet friend. And from Roarke's expression, it was clear he felt the importance of that offer to use her given name. "Bernadette," he said softly.

Valaria and Callum had been watching the exchange. And though Valaria didn't offer the same grace—not yet—Flora could see that this all had moved her. Her tone was gentle as she said, "Why don't we retire to the parlor and have port together? We can talk or play a game if you're up for it, Mr. Desmond."

"I'd like to try," Roarke said with a quick glance at Flora. "Though I think I might need some air first. Just to clear my head a little."

The other murmured their understanding and they began to depart to the salon where they would do their after-supper activities. Flora should have followed them, but instead she moved toward Roarke. "May I join you?"

He swallowed. She saw his Adam's apple work with the motion, saw his gaze flit over her, hot and a little possessive. She wanted to lean into that, into him, but managed to remain just where she was, as unaffected as she could pretend to be.

"Yes," he said. "Why don't you lead the way?"

She did so, taking him to the back of the estate, past the parlor where they could hear the others softly talking, probably about them, truth be told. They went through a small music room and out onto the large veranda that encircled the entire back of the house.

It was cold outside, and Flora shivered a little as the door closed behind them. She hadn't thought to fetch a wrap, even though it was autumn. She'd been too caught up in him.

"Here," he said, sweeping off his jacket. He stopped in front of her and gently placed it on her shoulders. The warmth of him permeated her, as if he were holding her, himself. And his scent had apparently been captured on the threads of Callum's coat, because she breathed him in with a soft sigh of pleasure.

"Thank you," she whispered.

He stood there with her a moment, his mouth opening and closing like he wanted to say something. Then he shook his head and walked to the edge of the veranda. He leaned on the waist-high wall and looked off into the distance, pensive and troubled.

She followed his stare and shivered. Out there was where they had been attacked. She moved to stand beside him, their hands almost touching on the wall's edge. "I hope I'll be able to see those woods as a positive place again one day in the future," she said.

He nodded slowly. "I hope that, too. I hope the past can be repaired."

She turned a little toward him. He was talking about them now. About their past. "Roarke," she said.

He looked at her, those green eyes piercing her. "Is there anything I can do?"

"Do?" she repeated.

"To make up for what I did. To show you how much you mean to me. I would go, if you like. I'd stay if you needed me. Just tell me and I'll do…anything. I would do anything."

He said it in a rush, the words tumbling from his mouth like he'd been holding them back. And perhaps he had, after all she had told him such a short time ago that she never wanted to see him again. That had never been true, of course.

She looked at their hands together on the veranda wall. Slowly, she eased her fingers out and traced his, gently. Their fingers wound together, tugging at each other, stroking and suddenly her whole body felt weightless. Hungry.

She blinked up at him, trying to find some level ground, but all he was to her now was shifting sands. He would draw her in and she would be lost. She *wanted* to be lost despite every good reason she had to back away. She could see she affected him, too. His pupils were dilated and it wasn't only because of the dim light. His breath was a little shorter, his body warm as he leaned toward her.

"Think about it." He lifted her hand to his lips and kissed it gently, sending another shock of desire tearing through her. "I'm not trying to pressure you."

Pressure. Oh yes, she felt that but not from him. She felt it from her own body, which throbbed in time to her own racing heartbeat. She felt it in the aching desire between her legs.

He motioned back toward the house. "Let's join the others, shall we?" he suggested.

She couldn't answer, but nodded mutely. As they entered the house, she slipped his jacket from her shoulders and handed it back. He shivered when he put it back on, just as she had. Like her body heat affected him as much as his had affected her.

They went to the parlor where the others were already drinking port and he smiled as he stepped in, the heated weight between them dissipating a fraction as he returned to friendly, easy guest with her friends.

"It was very kind of you to include me tonight," he said to Valaria and Callum. "I appreciate it more than you could ever know. But I do think I should rest, so I'll leave you four to your night if it isn't too rude of me."

"Of course," Valaria said, but there was no edge to her voice now. She seemed genuine, as if this time together tonight had softened even her to the man. "Please do rest. We have the instructions for tending to your wound and we can look at it tomorrow."

"Thank you," he said with a slight bow of his head to them, then to Bernadette. He turned toward Flora then and she stared up at him, memorizing every part of his face from the harsh angle of his jaw to the soft warmth of his green gaze to the bruise that said how much he was willing to sacrifice to save her. "Thank *you*," he repeated to her, touching her hand one last time, and then he left the room.

When he was gone she took a gulp of air she hadn't realized she needed and tried to school her features so she wouldn't be too obvious to her friends. From the way all three of them stared at her, she failed in that.

"I would love to continue hating him," Valaria said at last as she brought a glass of port over to Flora and handed it to her with a little smile. "But I can see that might only hurt you. So if you know what you intend to do about the man, I'll support whatever that is."

Flora drew back at the kindness of that suggestion. She knew Valaria was protective and she was lowering her guard for Flora's sake and nothing else. And yet she still had a great many questions. What she intended to do about Roarke in the long term was certainly one of them.

But what she intended to do about him tonight? Well, that had become crystal clear the moment he touched her hand that one final time, his warm breath stirring her lips, his gaze locked with hers and filled with meaning.

So all she had to do was wait until the right time. And hope he would accept her offer.

CHAPTER 19

Roarke had tried to sleep after he returned to his room, but he couldn't. He could only relive in shocking detail every moment he'd ever spent with Flora. He started, drawn from the fantasy when there was a knock on the door. He sat up. It was a hesitant knock, not certain like Callum's earlier or efficient like a servant's. His legs shook as he got to his feet and moved to open it.

Flora stood in the hallway, her auburn hair down around her shoulders, wrapped in a pale green silk robe that clung to every curve of her body. She stared up at him, blue eyes wide and filled with a desire that couldn't be mistaken. She licked her lips and those same eyes moved over him.

He was shirtless again, just as he had been earlier in the day, but he still wore Callum's borrowed trousers. Perhaps he had hoped she would come like this—if he were in his usual sleeping attire, naked, he wouldn't have been able to open the door to greet her.

"Roarke," she whispered. "I…I want…"

He caught her hand and drew her inside, pushing the door shut behind her as he slid his fingers into the waves of her gorgeous hair and tilted her face up to his. He kissed her and she seemed to melt against him instantly, all liquid desire and soft moan that vibrated against his lips. By God, how he wanted this woman, even if he didn't deserve her.

"Are you sure?" he murmured, breaking their lips just enough that he could speak, even though he didn't let her go, even though their mouths brushed even as he asked that question.

"Yes," she said, her tone strangled. "I want you. Please."

He nodded and kissed her again, deeper now, slower. She lifted against him, her silk-covered breasts rubbing against his bare chest. His fingers tightened against her back, almost against his will and he groaned into her mouth as tingles rushed through him. By God but this woman set him on fire. He'd never felt anything quite like it in his life. The fact that she was offering him another chance, even if it never went beyond this night, was a gift he couldn't quite fathom.

But he wanted it so desperately.

He drew back and looked down at her, drinking her in, marking every flush to her skin, every catch to her breath. He wanted to feel her flex in desire again, this time without lies or secrets between them. He wanted to steal this moment and hope he could leverage it into another and another and a million more.

"Are you well enough?" she whispered.

He realized she had taken him drinking her in as hesitation. He smiled. "My head feels much better, I assure you. But it could be falling off my neck and I would still do this. But just as before, I need you to know that you can say no at any point. Stop me at any time. There is not point of no return."

"I'm not going to stop you," she whispered, and then lowered her hands away from his arms and slowly untied her robe. She drew in a deep breath, as if she were girding herself for what would happen next, and then parted the folds of silk to reveal she was utterly, beautifully, entirely naked beneath.

And he was undone.

~

Sometimes Flora couldn't tell what Roarke was thinking when he stared at her. Hence why she'd never imagined he'd been lying to her before. But right now, in this moment, she could see every thought as if they were tattooed across his face. He looked down at her, standing before him naked and vulnerable, and there was only desire, only passion, only worship. She felt that and it weakened her that this man might worship her. She wanted him to, she wanted to worship him back.

"You've never seen me naked," she murmured. "No one has seen me naked save my maid for years."

He reached out and gently brushed the back of his hand across her shoulder, her collarbone, lower between her breasts, and she gasped with pleasure. "My God, but you are everything. I hardly know where to start with you like this."

She bit her lip as his knuckles gently smoothed across her right breast and nipple. "What you're doing right now is a good start," she gasped.

He smiled again, but this time it wasn't gentle or encouraging. There was something a little wild in that expression, a little feral, like he was holding back a beast and now it was threatening to break free. Oh, how she wanted to see that.

"Excellent," he said, and then bent his head to her. He kissed her throat, drawing her closer as he cupped her breast, stroking his thumb against her nipple with much more firmness.

She arched against him with a gasp of increasing pleasure. All she could think about was what he'd done with her in her parlor what felt like a lifetime ago. All she could think about was coming, but this time not just with his mouth or his fingers. She wanted him inside of her as she flexed and arched and begged.

If he sensed that building, heated, wanton desire, he made no move to slake it. He kept stroking her breast even as he glided his mouth to her bare shoulder, to nip the fine arch of her collarbone, then lower, lower until his tongue met his fingers at her nipple. He sucked and she jolted her hips against him, moaning his name as electric bursts of pleasure worked through every nerve ending.

He smiled up at her and then pulled away with a soft pop. "Why don't we lie on the bed?" he asked.

She nodded and took a few shaky steps to the edge of the high mattress. She was about to climb up and rest back against the pillows when he moved. He pressed against her from behind, his hands coming around to cup both breasts. She felt the hard ridge of his cock against her backside through his trousers and pushed against him on instinct.

He made a low, guttural groan against her ear and massaged her breasts harder, lifting and tugging and grinding against her all at once.

"Please," she whimpered, but instead of that making him just take her, he released her.

"On the bed," he ordered, but gently.

She did so and turned to find he was unfastening the trousers at last. She leaned up on her elbows, watching closely. If this was the first time he'd seen her naked, it was also her first time to see him the same. When he shed the heavy fabric in a pool at his feet, she caught her breath.

By God, but he was something. Thick like his thighs and already hard and curled against his flat stomach in readiness to claim. She reached out, hand trembling, and caught him, stroking him from base to tip. He dropped his head back with a pained groan and let her tug him for a moment before he caught her wrist and lifted her hand to his lips. He kissed her palm, that feral look in his eyes multiplied.

"As much as I like that, you are making me dizzy," he said with a chuckle. "Slide over."

She did so, watching him come into the bed. He rolled on his side to face her and she touched his cheek. "We could just lie together if you're—"

"Oh no," he said. "I'm not such an invalid that I can't do exactly what I cannot wait to do." He pushed back so he was seated in the bed and then motioned to her to his lap. "Please, Your Grace."

She hesitated a moment and then moved to straddle him, gripping his cock to align him to her body. But to her surprise, he pushed her hand away. "Not yet, sweet," he whispered. "I have so much more I want to do before I feel you take me."

She settled onto his lap, his cock against her backside, and leaned in, bracing her arms on the headrest on either side of him. He cupped the back of her neck and they kissed again. She lost herself in that kiss, in him, in his flavor, in the way he flexed beneath her, in the way her body changed beneath his touch.

His dragged his mouth back to her throat, back to her breast, massaging the right with his hand, sucking the left until she saw stars of pleasure. She dropped her head back, arching to offer him better access and surrendered to pleasure, to him.

And oh, what pleasure he offered, swirling his tongue, sucking gently, drawing his free hand down the apex of her body, until he found her thigh. She ground against him, hissing out her breath, longing for his touch as much as she'd ever longed for anything in her life.

He lifted his head from her breast and watched her as he smoothed two fingers against her sex, massaging her outer lips lightly. She jolted at the sensation and forced herself to lower her gaze to his, to hold there while he touched her, spread her, breached her wet body with one finger, then two.

"Roarke," she whimpered, and he nodded as he began to curl those same fingers inside, stimulating her as she rocked against him. His thumb found her clitoris and he teased it in time, building pleasure in her that bloomed and warmed her entire shaking body.

She wanted more. She wanted it all. When she found it, she dropped her head forward, muffling her moans against his shoulders as she flexed against his fingers in a never-ending waterfall of pleasure. When she had stopped twitching, he drew back, removing his fingers. He lifted them to his lips and licked them and she felt her body respond to that wicked action.

She felt herself wanting to do something just as wicked in return. She caught his hand and pulled it to her own mouth, tasting her release on his fingers as he stared at her in wild wonder.

"I think we've both waited long enough," he grunted, his voice harsh now, rough. He caught her hips and she squealed as he lifted her, maneuvered her. She reached between them, and this time he didn't push her away when she pressed the head of his cock against her entrance. All he did was moan her name as she slid down his length in one wet slide, filled completely by him.

It had been a long time since she done this. And it had never been like this. Never so wanton or desperate or filled with wild pleasure that seemed to rule every part of her quaking body. She couldn't wait, she couldn't be demure, she just needed to ride this man.

So she did, gripping his shoulders tightly as she began to rock and grind over him. He swore, his fingers digging harder into her hips, marking her, she hoped. She wanted to be marked by him, she wanted to mark him in return.

She cupped his cheeks, kissing him with all her passion as she rolled her hips over him. Their bodies slapped as they met and parted, a wet sound that aroused her even further, made her sink into the animalistic want that echoed through her entire being. He was hers, this was how she made him hers.

She nipped his lower lip and he rose harder in her from beneath with a heavy groan. And that sound of pleasure from this man who so obviously had far more experience than she did was enough to send ripples of pleasure to mount through her. She gripped him with her body, demanding more, taking it, and then she was soaring all over again, crying out without thought to who would hear. She didn't care. Let the house know she was well-pleasured. As long as he didn't stop.

And he didn't. He took her harder, faster, his hands digging into her thighs, his eyes wide as he watched her ride the crest of her pleasure. And only when she slid down the other side, her body weak with release and her mouth softer on his, did he lift against her few more times, pull from her body and spend between them in a hot gush of pleasure.

She rested her head against his shoulder, panting with exertion. His arms folded harder around her and he held her, smoothing his hands along her spine, his soft breath against her ear as he gently kissed any exposed skin he could find.

She lifted her head and looked at him. "Did I hurt you?"

He choked out a garbled laugh and shook his head. "I feel no pain, Flora, I promise you that. And if I do later, it is entirely worth it."

She smiled and kissed him once more before she slid from his lap and onto the bed next to him. He faced her, and they lay like that for she didn't know how long. Just watching each other, their fingers flexing along each other, measuring the other person's form.

Finally, she sighed. "I heard Callum saying that if a person has a blow to the head, it's sometimes good for them not to be alone afterward. Just the first night."

Both Roarke's eyebrows lifted and he winced. "Ugh, well, I can see why. I know there can be consequences to a blow to the head. Although I've only felt better in the hours since we were attacked."

She moved her hand to his chest and touched his pectoral, tracing the muscle there, then smoothing her fingers across his nipple and loving how he took in a sharp inhale. "Still," she said, holding his gaze. "Since you saved me, I think it might be best that I stay. Just to be certain. As long as that is something you would want."

His expression softened and he leaned into her, kissing her gently, then not so gently. He hardly parted his mouth from hers at all as he said, "I think you know best, Flora. I am at your mercy."

Then he kissed her even more deeply and soon proved that if anyone was at anyone's mercy, it was her. And she couldn't have been happier in that knowledge.

CHAPTER 20

The next two days seemed to fly by for Flora. Despite the threats against her and Roarke recovering from his injuries, the time they shared was magical. When they were with her friends, he was pleasant and interesting, and she could see them all slowly coming to forgiveness for what he'd done. Even Valaria smiled more often at him now and no longer glared.

As for her, he was always honest, always direct. And when they were alone, even more so. She'd learned more about his father, his mother. They'd even talked about Stuart. The fact that he'd cared about a person she'd loved only seemed to bring them more together.

And at night? Well, those times were even better. Roarke might still be bruised and his stitches still red and swollen, but he was certainly capable of passion. He made love to her over and over, drawing pleasure from her in ways she hadn't even known were possible. Then they'd lie together afterward, whispering about the future, about the past, about anything at all before he swept her up and started all over again.

She was falling head over heels in love with him. She hadn't said so yet. The uncertainty his lies had created weeks ago remained around her heart and she didn't want to jump too soon and put herself in an even worse position. But when she pictured her life, she was having a harder and harder time picturing it without him.

Even now, she sat across from him in the parlor, watching him read a book while Bernadette played the piano and sang for them as Valaria and Callum playfully danced and laughed, and she could see a lifetime like this. With good friends and easy times and pleasure.

There was a light knock on the parlor door, and everyone looked up at once as Callum's butler entered the chamber. "Excuse me, Your Graces, Mr. Desmond."

Callum moved toward him a step. "Not at all. What is it, Mitchell?"

"Two letters have arrived," he said, and held out the missives. "One for Mr. Desmond and one for the Duchess of Tunbridge."

Roarke and Bernadette exchanged a glance and then Bernadette got up from the pianoforte so they could walk to Mitchell together.

"Who could have..." Bernadette began, and then her face lit up. "Oh, it's Theo's handwriting on both."

Roarke's expression grew sharper and he almost snatched the letter away, tearing it open and reading it with shaking hands. Flora went to him, resting a hand on his back. "He reached London and your mother."

Roarke nodded. "Yes. He says she is well and he has moved her to his London estate temporarily. It seems her companion, Hilde, was approached by my cousins just before his arrival. They were harassed." He was pale as paper. "But Mama is safe now."

She heard the waver in his voice and stared at him. This man, who was so strong, so decent, had been torn apart in the last few years by circumstance and mistakes and the horrible nature of his cousins. And while the first things were not related to her, the last certainly was. He had been used as a weapon because her stepchildren were focused on her as a target.

Everything she needed to do became crystal clear in that moment.

"We need to go back to London," she said, her tone firm and even. "We all do. It's time we face this head on and free us all from this terror."

Roarke turned on her, the pages of Theo's letter fluttering to the ground at his feet. He had a fearful look on his face that broke her heart even further. "Absolutely not."

Callum stepped forward. "I tend to agree with Roarke. Going back to London seems an unnecessary risk for you, Flora. The rest of us can go and you can remain safely here while we—"

She stared at him and then back at Roarke. "You cannot be serious in that suggestion. You think I would remain here doing, what? Crocheting, strolling the dead garden in the rain like a gothic heroine with armed servants trailing me? While you face off with people who apparently want *me* dead?"

"*Because* they want you dead," Roarke said. "And have tried to actually fulfill that desire not three days ago. That is why, yes, you should stay here."

Frustration rose in her, spreading through her chest, and she folded her arms and glared at him. "And just what do you think you and Callum and Theo can do when you ride in on your horses with capes flowing behind you heroically? My stepchildren have proven they don't give a damn about anything but keeping the inheritance they believe will be wrongly bestowed upon me. Nothing you three can say or do will change that. And they will only become more desperate as the anniversary of their father's death grows nearer."

Roarke opened and shut his mouth and looked at Callum, who shrugged. They couldn't argue with the truth in the end. She knew it and so did they.

She caught Roarke's hands and held them both, pulling his attention back to her and her only. "This will not end, none of us can be free, until *I* resolve things with my stepchildren once and for all." He opened his mouth again, but she cut him off before he could start. "You will be with me, Roarke. Certainly we will need to arrange the safest situation for this to happen, I don't disagree. But in the end, I must face this dragon. And I must slay it myself."

"This isn't a fairytale," Roarke said with a shake of his head that showed his frustration matched her own. He released her hands and stepped back. "I've known the three of them much longer than you have and I've heard the way they look and sound when they talk about you. If you try to face them head on, you'll be strolling into a viper's den. I can't be a part of that."

She blinked as she looked up at him, saw his fear on her behalf slashed across his expression. "Then don't be."

Valaria caught her breath across the room, and Callum stepped back to offer them space as Roarke recoiled slightly. "What?"

Her chest hurt but she forced herself to continue, "They dragged you into this mess, but it's because of me. Because of *my* relationship with their father. Because they feel I took something from them."

"I'm not sending you off alone to them!" he said, his voice elevating.

She drew in a long breath. "You say you don't want to be there for this, but you don't want me to be alone. And it's not fair, but you must choose one. Because I'm not asking your permission, Roarke. I spent my life doing that. Asking my father, asking my husband. I can't ask anymore. For the first time since Stuart's death, I *know* what to do. Both for myself and for you. And it feels good, even if I'm afraid. Please don't take that away from me."

He stared at her, his eyes wide and wild, filled with pain she wished desperately she could assuage. "I lost you once," he said. "Because I made a mistake. And the idea that I might make another one and lose you again, lose you permanently, that would be too much to bear." He took her hand. "I'm not sure you comprehend their hatred for you."

"A man tried to kill me," she whispered. "And I watched him try to kill you. Don't underestimate me."

He shut his eyes and let her go. "I never would. Not you or

them." He backed up. "I'd be a fool to think I could change your mind or that I've earned the right to do so. I just hope your friends will talk you into actions more sensible."

With that he turned and left the room. Left her feeling empty, but not unsure.

"Flora," Callum said softly.

She shook her head without looking at him. "If he couldn't convince me, neither can you. I will face off with them at last. If you all love me, you'll just help me figure out how to do it as safely as possible. Even if Roarke is unable to stand by my side."

Roarke hadn't rejoined the party after Flora's announcement that she would face off with her stepchildren. And she hadn't joined him in his bed that night. But the lot of them had loaded up in carriages and on horses the next morning and were now making the day and a half trip back to London.

Roarke rode alongside Valaria and Callum's carriage. Inside were Valaria, Bernadette and Flora. Sometimes he saw Flora push back the curtain and look at him, her expression unreadable.

He tried to make his the same.

Callum eased his horse up beside Roarke and cleared his throat. Roarke gave him a side glance. His friend had joined him riding outside twenty minutes before but hadn't said anything much beyond casual conversation about the roads. This was clearly not going to be a conversation about that.

"You look sick," Callum said gently. "It is troubling that you would ride yourself to pain rather than just talk to her."

"I tried to talk to her yesterday," Roarke said through clenched teeth. "What more could I say?"

"That you respect her. That you support her. That you love her. I think that's all she needs to hear." Callum shook his head. "You are at a crossroads, my friend. I hate to see you make the wrong decision and perhaps keep yourself from a happy future. Keep her from the same."

"And what is the right decision?"

"Stand by her. You'll certainly have the best chance of protecting her, if nothing else."

Roarke didn't respond for a moment, but let those words roll around in his head. Finally he glared at Callum. "Were you always so annoyingly correct, Blackvale?"

Callum laughed. "Since birth, I'm afraid."

Roarke looked at the carriage again and sighed. "I'm certain you must want to ride with your future wife and Bernadette. I wonder if I could convince Flora to ride in private with me in her carriage. It's empty, yes?"

"Yes, the servants are in the first carriage up ahead," Callum said. "And I think that's a wonderful idea." He lifted a hand and motioned for their caravan to stop.

There was much jockeying as everyone got out and stretched their backs, drank cold tea from jugs and talked. Flora stood to the side, watching him and Roarke drew a long breath before he sidled up to her.

"Will you ride with me in your carriage for a while?" he asked. "I'm feeling the need for a break from riding and it will be too crowded if we're all in Blackvale's rig."

She nodded. "Of course. Are you well?"

He smiled at her concern. She might be annoyed with him, uncertain, but she was still so kind. It was her nature to her core and he adored her even more for that. It was something to emulate.

"I am," he assured her. "But I do…I do miss you. Even after just one night apart."

"I missed you, too," she whispered as she reached out to take his hand. She squeezed it gently before she said, "I'll tell the others the plan if you want to meet me at the carriage."

He watched her go, drank her in as she talked to her friends for a moment. She smiled and it was like someone had lit up the dreary day. What a thing that would be to have in one's life forever. He hoped he might one day have that chance as he walked to her carriage, parked now behind Blackvale's.

She returned to him and he helped her up. They took places across from each other, silent in the midst of the sounds of everyone else going back to their rigs and servants mounting horses and their party starting back on their way.

It was only when they had started moving that he cleared his throat. "I'm sorry."

She blinked. "Oh."

"I feel like that is all I ever say to you and I hate that it's where we must begin." He shook his head. "I-I couldn't protect my mother my entire childhood. I loved my father, you know that. But he was unreliable. His mistakes and missteps made her life harder, and I wanted so desperately to make it easier."

"You were a child," she said softly.

"I know. And I wouldn't expect any other child to do the same now." He sighed. "But I still felt as though it was my duty to shield her. To the worst ends, as you know. I suppose, though, that it taught me to be protective of everyone I care about. That it is my duty to be so. And my resistance to your plans is because of that, not because I doubt their veracity or your capacity to handle yourself. You are brilliant and strong and resilient. I have no doubt you can win any fight you enter."

Her lips parted. "I…no one has ever seen me that way."

"I do," he said. "You will fight with kindness, with compassion, with wisdom. And I…I would be honored to stand beside you as you do, if you still want me there. I trust your instincts, even if I cannot entirely school my terror at what might happen."

Her expression had softened and she reached across the carriage for his hand. Their fingers threaded together and an enormous sense of peace flooded him. Like weights lifted from his shoulders. He was, as always, awed by that fact.

"If I could only have one champion at my side when I face them, it would be you," she whispered. "Only you. Always you."

She moved to his side of the rig then, settling in beside him and wrapping her arms around him. Her mouth was tilted up and he couldn't resist. He took it, kissing her and feeling like it had been a lifetime since he'd done so, even though it was only a day.

She murmured against his lips, her fingers tightening around his back. She pulled back a fraction. "Before we arrange this meeting, though, I want to do one other thing."

"What's that?" he asked.

"Meet your mother," she said. "If you'd allow me."

"Yes," he said without hesitation. "I would very much want you to meet her. But I don't think we should talk about her right now."

"And why is that?" she asked.

"Because I don't want to be thinking about her while I do what I'm about to do," he said, letting his hands glide down her shoulders, cup her breast.

She smiled and her pupils dilated with desire. "And what is that?"

He didn't answer, but dropped to his knees on the carriage floor at her feet. He pushed her skirt, lifting it over her calves, her knees, up to her thighs. She scooted down on the carriage bench, widening her legs to allow him access.

He murmured his approval as he brushed his cheek against her inner thigh. He could already scent her desire and it drove him wild, as did the little gasp of pleasure when his fingers slid up and he teased her sex gently.

"Roarke," she whispered, the broken sound of it like music to his ears.

He pressed his mouth to her as he spread her open and she lifted to meet his tongue. They danced this dance, as they had before, him tasting and teasing, sucking and licking, her rising and falling in time, gripping one hand in his hair and one along the edge of the carriage seat.

He did not waste a moment—he wanted to make her come, to

feel her come, taste her come, to reform whatever bonds had been frayed by their disagreement. She seemed to want the same. She held her gaze on him as he worked at her, whispering and whimpering his name, focused on him as he focused on her.

When she came, it was as magnificent as ever. Her sex rippled and flexed, her cries were loud in the quiet of the small space. He reveled in every moment, every sound, every flavor of her. He memorized each one because they meant so much to him. And he never wanted to forget that, no matter what transpired next.

He couldn't.

Flora's body felt weightless as she came down from the high of Roarke pleasuring her. She'd never thought to do something so wicked in a carriage, practically a public place, but it had been arousing and exciting to watch him go down on his knees for her and match the rolling rhythm of the carriage to bring her to the pinnacle of pleasure.

She tugged his hair gently and drew him to lean up her body. He caged either side of her head with the flat of his palms on the carriage wall and smiled before she kissed him. He tasted of her. Of her need, of her pleasure. He tasted of his own need, unslaked at this point.

She wanted to change that.

"I want you," she whispered against his mouth. "Inside of me." His eyes went wide and he stared at her as if he weren't certain. She wanted to make him certain, so she dropped her hand between them and unfastened the fall front of his trousers. When it fell away, his hard cock pushed free into her hand. She stroked him once, twice. "Please."

He made a garbled sound at that and cupped her backside with both hands beneath her gown. She buried her head into his neck as he aligned their bodies and took her with one long, smooth stroke.

She was so sensitive from her earlier orgasm that every slide of him was heaven. She ground up, rubbing her clitoris against his pelvis every time he fully filled her and soon enough she was on the edge again.

She cupped his cheeks and kissed him deeper, harder as she shattered around him. He gasped against her tongue, her name like a plea and a surrender that took her orgasm to new heights.

And then he was gone, pulling from her to spend against his hand as he cursed until she blushed. He dropped his forehead to hers, and for a little while they just panted together, hands still smoothing along the lines of the other, pleasure still flowing between them like a current.

She never wanted to break that connection, she wanted to stay in this fantasy world forever, bound only by pleasure to his remarkable man.

But they would be in London soon. And she couldn't truly start her future, whatever that might be, until she resolved her past. Even if that meant putting herself in danger to do so.

CHAPTER 21

Flora had felt Roarke's anxiety before. It had been evident when he told her about the lies he'd used against her, about his relationship to her stepchildren. And again after the attack, when he couldn't hide his terror on her behalf, even when he was injured.

But now, sitting in Theo's parlor in London just a short time after their party's arrival in the city, she felt it pulsing through him like a heartbeat. While she sat on the settee, hands folded in her lap, he paced the room, unable to stay still as he watched the door and waited for the arrival of his mother.

Flora didn't know what to expect. He'd told her about Mrs. Desmond, of course. And he'd reminded Flora that she was not clear of mind even as they arrived. But now the door to the parlor opened and a small, frail woman was led in by a taller lady with a sweet, kind face.

Flora rose and caught her breath. Theo's bright green gaze had come from his mother. Seeing his eyes on her face immediately made Flora feel warmly toward her, but she held back in her greeting. She didn't want to confuse Mrs. Desmond any more than she already seemed to be as she looked around the room, her brow furrowing with concern.

"Where are we, Hilde?" she asked, and Flora's heart broke as she watched Roarke's smile fall slightly.

"We're still in the Duke of Lightmorrow's home, Mrs. Desmond," Hilde said with an apologetic look for both Roarke and her. "Remember, he's so kindly let us stay here the last few days."

Mrs. Desmond's brow wrinkled a little and she nodded. "Oh."

"Look who is here," Hilde said.

Roarke stepped forward and Hilde's face fell at his bruised countenance. It made Flora look more closely at it. His purple bruises were beginning to heal, but there was no doubt he'd been injured in a grievous fight. He made no mention of it but said, "Good afternoon, Mama, Hilde. May I present the Duchess of Sidmouth?"

Hilde seemed to have pulled herself together as she gave a brief curtsey in Flora's direction. "Good afternoon, Your Grace."

"Good afternoon," she said back, and then she moved toward Roarke's mother. "And Mrs. Desmond. I have heard so many lovely things about you from your son. I'm so pleased to make your acquaintance at last."

Though Mrs. Desmond didn't seem to fully comprehend that statement, she held out a hand regardless. "You are very pretty."

Flora took her hand and gently guided her to the settee. "Oh, you're too kind. May I get you some tea?" Hilde glanced at her and Flora nodded. "I assume you might wish to talk to Roarke a moment."

Roarke swallowed. "But—"

"We'll be fine," Flora assured him gently. "Speak with Hilde."

Roarke held her gaze a moment and then motioned Hilde into the hallway. As he left, Flora turned back to his mother. "How do you take it?"

"Two sugar and lots of milk," Mrs. Desmond said.

"Excellent, I like my tea extra sweet also. And I see that the duke's people put out some wonderful biscuits. Raspberry is my favorite—would you like some of those, as well?"

Mrs. Desmond nodded, and Flora went about the business of

preparing the tea. She came back and sat next to her companion, examining her closely. She looked tired, and Flora wished in that moment that she could do everything in the world to make her comfortable and safe. Not just for Roarke, although knowing she could protect someone he loved so deeply was all she could wish to do.

But just for this lady herself, who hadn't earned this difficult time.

Flora took her hand gently. "I've heard you have a son, is that right?"

Just as she suspected, Mrs. Desmond made no glance toward the door where Roarke had gone. She didn't recall who he was, and it was heartbreaking. "Yes, little Roarke. He's just five, you know."

"Is he," Flora said, and blinked at tears. "What a lovely age. I'd like to hear all about him."

And so Mrs. Desmond told her everything about Roarke as a little boy, about her husband the dreamer, about their life together. And Flora listened to it all in rapture…and tried not to cry.

As Roarke stepped into the hallway with Hilde, he drew in an unsteady breath. "I was told you were harassed while I was in the countryside."

Hilde's eyes filled with tears and she wobbled a bit before she said, "Yes. I was walking with your mother in the park by the house. When she's able, I try to take her to get air as often as possible. We had entered a quiet part by a pond she likes when your cousin showed up."

Roarke tensed, his hands gripping at his sides. "Which one?"

"Not the duke," she said. "The—the other one. I don't know his name."

"Philip," Roarke murmured. So, Thomas had made his younger brother his weapon not once, but twice. And it seemed Philip took his duties very seriously, though of course he would. He'd always been short-tempered and ready to bruise to make a point. "What did he do?"

"He raced up, screaming at me, screaming at her. He told me he could have things...done to my son? He's trying to find a place in the army, you see, since he can't work. Your cousin said he could have him booted out or worse." Now the tears flowed. "He was hateful. Your mother was weeping, I was shaking and trying to get away from him. He shouted us all the way into the house with the neighbors staring before he got into a carriage with the ducal crest and thundered off."

Roarke shut his eyes. "It's my fault."

Hilde stepped closer and shook her head. "It isn't, sir. I know you would have done anything to prevent that from happening."

"But I didn't," he said. "Not enough at any rate."

Hilde cleared her throat. "What happened to you, sir?"

Roarke knew what she meant. He'd seen her reaction to his bruised face when she came into the room with his mother. He wanted to lie to her, to reassure her...but he knew from recent experience that it wouldn't make things better. And he owed more to this woman who had served his mother and never complained about his lack of funds.

"My cousins send someone to attack the duchess," he admitted softly. "And I intervened. The bruises are the result."

Now Hilde's expression crumpled. "So they aren't empty threats."

"Perhaps not. I'm so sorry you were frightened," Roarke said as Hilde gripped his hand, the horror in her gaze real. "I should have been more prepared—I didn't know how far my cousins would go."

"I adore your mother, sir, I do," Hilde said. "But I can't—"

"I know," he said, trying not to panic. "And I promise you that I'll do everything in my power to get this situation rectified. But if you feel you must leave my employ...I'll figure something out."

Hilde drew a long breath. "I'll have to think on it. At least here it feels safe. His Grace has been nothing but kind, especially to your mother."

Roarke bent his head. "And I can never repay him for that, though I will surely try. I'm glad this time here has been a respite for you. I think it will be a few days more until we resolve things with my cousins. Then we can talk about the future."

Of course, at present he couldn't picture the future. Not for his mother, not for himself, not for Flora. It all felt in the air, dark and frightening and growing more so with every time he saw how far his cousins would go to protect their money.

The door to the parlor opened and Flora stepped out. "She's a bit tired, I think. Overwhelmed by meeting someone new."

"Yes," Hilde said, wiping her tears. "Of course. I'll join her and help her finish, then get her up to bed for a rest."

After Hilde had gone back into the parlor, Flora stepped closer. "She's lovely. Your mother, I mean. And—"

"I love you," he interrupted.

She blinked up at him, her expression turning from one of comfort to surprise. "Wh-what?"

"I love you, Flora," he continued, even though he hadn't meant to start this conversation here in a hallway in another man's house. "I love you with all my heart, even though I know full-well that I don't deserve you. This time with you, watching her with you, becoming more and more aware of the threat against us all...I need you to know it."

She was silent a moment, just staring at him. Then she moved closer. His heart had begun to race and he tried to keep himself level. She might deny him and he had to accept that when it happened.

She cupped his cheeks in both hands, her thumbs smoothing along his jaw gently. "I love you, Roarke," she whispered.

For a moment, nothing else in the world existed. There were no sounds above the rushing of his blood in his veins, nothing to see but her beautiful face staring up at him, no light but her light, which pierced through the darkness like a beacon home.

"You...love me?" he whispered. "Even after everything I—"

"I don't have to love everything you do to love you," she said. "You've apologized and worked to prove yourself. And after seeing your mother, hearing her talk about you, it's obvious you would have done anything for her." She looked back over her shoulder toward the parlor. "And now so would I. She deserves protection. So do you."

He almost buckled at those words. He'd spent a great many years without anyone to protect or care for him, and now this remarkable woman offered both. She offered her heart, which was worth twenty times the amount of money his cousins were willing to kill for.

He sighed. "Well, that protection is something we need to work out quickly," he said. "Philip did more than harass my mother and Hilde. He threatened them."

The color went out of her face and her hands began to shake even as she rested them on his arms. "Wh-what?"

He nodded. "They're safe here with Theo for the time being. But this must be resolved. And I think...as much as I hate it...that you might be right you are the only one who can end this."

She let out a shaky breath. "We can. Together. Come, the others are in the east parlor waiting for us. Why don't we join them? And we can figure out together exactly what to do and how to do it. Because I want to fight for our future, Roarke."

He pulled her closer, folded his arms around her, breathed in the soft scent of her hair and reveled in the warmth of her embrace. "So do I," he said.

And for the first time in the long time, the future felt like something worth fighting for.

"Your mother's companion played down the threat," Theo said with a shake of his head a short while later. "I understand why, as she doesn't know me well. But if these people were willing to go so far…"

Flora sighed. They'd been going around and around this subject for twenty minutes. Since Theo hadn't been present when she'd declared she would face off with her stepchildren, they'd been having the same conversation over again to convince him.

"If you don't want them to meet with me here," she said gently, "I understand. Callum, would you allow me to use your home instead? Mine is so small and it will feel unprotected. I want my stepchildren to see that I have powerful allies."

Theo's jaw tightened as he glanced at Bernadette. She stared right back at him and moved closer a step. "Theo," she said softly. "Please."

All at once, his doubt seemed to fade. He dipped his head and said, "Of course I will allow you to do this here if you insist. But I want protections in place. Guards at the ready. And I think Bernadette shouldn't be here." He paused. "Or Valaria."

But anyone could see that Valaria was nothing more than an afterthought. She even smothered a smile into her palm before she said, "As much as I appreciate your gallantry, Bernadette and I both want to be here. We might not be in the room, but we can be with Mrs. Desmond and Hilde, as a distraction, if nothing else. And as support for Flora when this is finished."

Theo rolled his eyes and paced off, his hands clenched at his sides. Callum followed him and the two talked quietly by the fireplace for a moment.

"He's going to allow it," Roarke said as he placed an arm around Flora's waist. She melted into his side a little and looked up at him. She was still spinning from his declaration of love a short time ago. How she wished she could only celebrate that joyous connection rather than have to plan to sever a much more unpleasant one.

"I hate that we must put them in this position," she murmured. "All of them."

"They'd do anything for you," Roarke said, and then leaned down to kiss her cheek. "And so would I."

She looked over to find her friends all staring at her. At them. She cleared her throat. "Roarke and I are together," she said with a shrug. "Truly together. And if Valaria and Callum are going to sneak kisses, then I demand the same allowance."

She paused and waited to see if they would argue or laugh at her teasing. Relief filled her when all of them smiled. "Duly noted," Callum said.

"Let's get our plans set," Theo added, and he touched Bernadette's hand quickly as he passed by her and stopped in front of Roarke and Flora. "The first step is to invite those monsters here. As soon as possible. And then we have to decide what you're going to say."

"I know what I'm going to say," Flora said, pushing her shoulders back. "So all I need now is a quill and paper. I want to finish this." She glanced over at Roarke. "Because I'm very much looking forward to what comes next."

CHAPTER 22

Flora had felt certain when she penned her brusque, direct note to Thomas and his siblings the previous day. But from that moment on her confidence had faded, replaced with fears. At least she hadn't had to face them alone. She had remained at Theo's the night before and Roarke had stayed with her. They'd shared a bed but hadn't made love, just held each other and talked about what would happen once her stepchildren arrived.

They hadn't, she'd noticed, talked about after. Perhaps because until this was resolved, it was too terrifying to consider what could be taken from them.

Now she paced the parlor. Roarke, Callum and Theo stood at the fireplace, talking softly together. Roarke looked at her from time to time, holding her gaze, drawing a deep breath so she would do the same. A comfort without even touching her.

There was a knock at the door out in the foyer and she froze, her hands shaking as she listened to Theo's butler welcome their very much unwelcome guests. She recognized their voices as they came closer up the hall, even though she had not heard them for years. The children hadn't included her in anything once she'd moved to Kent's Row.

"The Duke of Sidmouth," Theo's butler said, and Flora jolted a little. She would never become accustomed to the fact that Thomas was duke now, not his father. No matter how many years Stuart was gone. "And Lord Philip and Lady Gertrude," the butler continued.

He stepped back and the three entered. It was like a storm blew in when they stepped into the room, everything felt darker and laced with more tension. Flora stared at them in their peacock finery, looking down their collective noses at her. Three years gone and all of them looked older, their cruelty aging them at a faster rate. Gertrude was only a little bit older than Flora, but she looked ten years her senior. Thomas still looked down his nose at her like she was a bit of shite on his boot.

It was Philip who made her shiver. Philip who she knew had been the one to orchestrate the attack on her in the country. Philip who had always haunted her steps when she was married to his father, making her uncomfortable with his intense regard. Now he looked her up and down with hatred that burned in his eyes like an inferno.

"Good afternoon," Theo said, his tone taut and very much unwelcoming. "Thank you for joining us."

Thomas looked at Theo, then Callum, then Roarke, and smirked. "A whole army of men to protect you, is it, Flora? It seems my thoughts on your virtue were correct."

Roarke made a move toward his cousin, but Callum caught his arm and held him steady. Flora stood slightly in front of him as she held Thomas's gaze evenly. "I think I need a guard after you all tried to kill me."

Thomas's brow wrinkled and he looked genuinely confused. Gertrude didn't, of course, as she had reported the plan to Roarke. She dropped her chin and stared at the ground beneath her feet. But Philip smiled, and it was terrifying.

"Kill you?" Thomas repeated.

Flora glanced up at Roarke and could see he was considering

this response just as she was. Did the duke truly not know what had happened?

"If you want to talk to us, *Flora,*" Philip said with a smirk, "then why don't you talk to us rather than hiding behind these people?"

"I would not have a guest in my home threatened," Theo said evenly. All the teasing and playfulness that he normally carried on his face and in his tone was gone now. This was a man not to be trifled with. "Blackvale and I will step to the other side of the room if you require privacy, we aren't leaving, Your Grace." He arched a brow at Thomas. "And we will not have this discussion again."

"Very well," Thomas said, waving the dukes off and following when Flora motioned their group toward a section of the room beside the window. It looked down over the garden far below and yet she took no comfort in the light and airy expanse.

She folded her arms. "Let me begin by saying that I know what you have done. What you demanded Roarke do in order to hurt me. And all for money." She glared at them. "Your father would be so disappointed in you all."

Thomas and Gertrude at least had the decency to blanche at her statement. Philip only seemed to seethe further.

"Whatever you think we've done—" Thomas began, effecting a tone of boredom.

She waved her hand to interrupt him, fully embracing her role as duchess for as long as she retained it. "You asked Roarke to sleep with me in order to withhold an additional inheritance I knew nothing about." She arched a brow. "Come now, own your behavior proudly. I've heard you did so before you were looking me in the face."

Thomas pursed his lips. "My father was under a spell when he made that amendment to his financial arrangements. We were only trying to protect what is ours."

"Of course you were," Flora said. "And you would go so far as to send an attacker after me in the countryside."

"You've accused me of attempted murder twice, Flora, and I

don't know what you're talking about," Thomas said. "Did I have intentions to stop you? Yes. But not through those means. If you are being dramatic for effect—"

"How do you think your cousin got those bruises? That cut across his forehead, which will scar?" she snapped. "Defending me, as he is twice the man either of you has ever been."

Thomas glanced at Roarke, who nodded. She could feel him leaning forward, she could feel him just barely keeping himself from beating both his cousins to a pulp. She reached back and took his hand gently.

"He was going to stab her," Roarke said, his voice shaking, "when I came flying out of the woods to stop him. The brute nearly killed me instead."

"That…that cannot be true," Thomas said. "I didn't arrange such a thing."

"Philip did," Gertrude said, hardly over a peep.

The group looked at her en masse. Her cheeks were bright red, her hands were shaking and she wouldn't look at any of them.

"I-I heard him making the plans," she continued.

Philip moved on her, striking her across the cheek with the back of his hand so quickly that no one could stop him. "Shut your mouth, Gertrude," he snapped.

"That's enough!" Callum barked, moving from the other side of the room toward them, Theo on his heels.

Philip watched them, then looked at Thomas, Roarke and Flora. He seemed to weigh his options, and then he grabbed his sister and tugged her hard against his chest, wrapping an arm around her neck as she squealed and scratched to get free.

"You're going to lay this on me, are you?" he asked, glaring at Thomas. "You told me to do anything necessary to get rid of the problem."

"I didn't mean murder!" Thomas gasped out. "Let Gertrude go, Philip. That's enough."

"*She* took everything," Philip continued, backing around the edge of the room against the wall so he couldn't be taken from behind. "That whore took everything from us, and she won't take another thing. I did the right thing, Thomas. And when I found out that bastard failed? Well, he had to be handled too."

Roarke reached forward and caught Flora's arm, gently pushing her behind him. "You killed him?"

"He was expendable," Philip said. "I'll have to find someone else."

"No!" Thomas said, his face a true mask of horror. In that moment, Flora believed him that he hadn't intended for this kind of physical harm to come to her. Other kinds, perhaps, but not murder.

"Let your sister go," Theo said evenly.

"Yes, please, Philip," Roarke said softly. "You must not want to hurt your family."

"Look at the duke," Philip sneered as he glared at his brother. "He'll throw me to the wolves now. Just like he always did when we were growing up. Asked me to do his dirty work and then ran to our father the moment it looked like there would be consequences. I won't suffer them, not for you."

Thomas glanced at Flora and she shook her head as she said to him, "Tell your brother that you'll protect him. Tell him we'll work it out."

Philip barked out a laugh. "God, even the whore is defending me. But not you, eh? You just wanted to benefit from my work, not claim it to get your hands dirty. Well, I'm about to solve your problem, *brother*. Only I know it will create a great many more issues in the end."

He had been moving the entire time he was speaking, and now he positioned himself right in front of the huge window. With a wild smile, he lunged backward and crashed through the glass.

Roarke lunged as he did so, catching Gertrude around the waist, and the three of them staggered and jerked through the broken window toward the hard paved squares of the garden patio beneath, with its statuary scattered throughout.

Flora screamed and jolted toward Roarke, but Callum and Theo reached him first, catching him, catching Gertrude before Philip's grip slipped and he tumbled out of view and landed with a horrific crunching thud beneath. Without his weight to pull them, the others fell back into the room, panting and grunting with the exertion.

Immediately Gertrude began to weep, and Thomas kept drawing in heaving breaths as he and Flora stepped to the edge of the broken window and looked down at the twisted, unmoving body below.

Thomas stared at his dead brother, whose blood had begun to pool on the ground around him, then at his sister, whose neck was already starting to bruise as she wept in Theo's arms, and finally at Flora as she rushed to Roarke and fell into his embrace, checking to make sure he hadn't been injured, yet again, by the machinations of those who so hated her.

"What have I done?" the new duke whispered, his voice breaking. "My God, what have I done?"

It took some time for the situation to calm itself. A doctor was called, though it was far too late for Philip. He checked on Gertrude and gave her something to help her rest before she was escorted home by servants. Thomas stayed, silent and staring with empty eyes as his brother's body was taken. As the servants scrubbed away the blood Philip had left behind.

Roarke clung to Flora the entire time. She no longer trembled in his arms, though occasionally she looked up at him and whispered, "He could have taken you with him."

And he reassured her and tried not to think of exactly that. Or what would have happened if Philip had grabbed for Flora instead of Gertrude for his last grasp at escape from his actions. But finally all the outsiders were gone and all that was left was their friend circle and Thomas.

Thomas shook his head. "I imagine you cannot believe me after everything that happened, but I never wanted this."

"No," Flora said, stepping from Roarke's arms at last. Even with her hair tangled and her cheeks streaked with tears, she looked so strong and brave in that moment. And oh, how he loved her. "No, you wanted me ruined or even raped, but not this. *This* was too far for you."

Thomas winced as his plans were thrown in his face. As they seemed to sink in. "You were right when you said that my father would hate me for what I wanted to do. And for what my insistence in dragging in Philip, who I knew was unstable, did do."

Flora's expression softened slightly and she shook her head. "Despite your multitude of faults, Thomas, your father adored you and your siblings. He kept hoping you could get over your hatred of me. He would be disappointed. But he loved you."

Roarke flinched at the way Thomas's face broke at that kindness that he hadn't earned. Would soon forget as he swept all this under a very large rug and moved on in the position he had fought for, with the money he had very nearly killed for, at least by proxy.

"I will not contest the additional inheritance," Thomas said at last.

Flora wrinkled her brow. "When I called you here, I was going to tell you that I didn't want it. I renounce it, Thomas."

His face twisted. "What?"

"You assume that everyone is so greedy as you three were," she said with a glance at Roarke. "But I received more than enough for my comfort. And what matters most to me as a legacy of your father is that we loved each other. I will never forget that or lose it, even as I move on to a new future. So keep your money. Or better yet, pay Roarke what you had offered to give him to betray me. You used him and hurt him. Perhaps that is better recompense."

Roarke caught his breath. "I-I don't want the money. It's blood money."

Thomas was silent for a long time as he stared at Roarke. "As children I think we sometimes cared for each other, didn't we?"

Roarke nodded. "Yes. I didn't always like you, but I cared for you and for my uncle and aunt."

"You saved my sister's life," Thomas said. "So I will gladly give you five thousand pounds for that. And I assume it will be the last time we speak, as I cannot have earned any further consideration from a man who it turns out is worth a great deal more than I am. Title and all." Thomas smoothed his wrinkled clothing and then the softness left his expression. "It will be in your account in a few days, Desmond. Do with it and with your future what you will. Good day."

He turned then and left without acknowledging anyone, without any other farewell. He left and Roarke knew that he would never see that part of his family again.

He turned toward Flora and stared first at her and then at their friends. "That is not the way I wanted to earn a fortune," he murmured.

Callum smiled and stepped forward to slap his shoulder. "Then you better do good things with it. Come, Valaria, Theo, Bernadette. Let's leave these two for a moment. I think they must have a great deal to say to each other."

Roarke didn't look at them anymore. He put all his focus on Flora as they all left and shut the door behind them, leaving them alone.

And then he said the only thing he could.

"Flora, will you marry me?"

Flora stared at Roarke, uncertain if she had dreamed those words or if they were real.

"This is not the best of circumstances," he said, his voice shaking a little. "Considering what we all went through today. But I couldn't wait one more moment."

She reached out to take his hand and looked up into his bruised face. He bore the marks of how far he'd go to protect her. To how he would love her for the rest of their lives if she said yes.

"This was a terrible day," she whispered. "But perhaps that makes this the perfect time. We never know what could happen from one moment to the next, do we? Loss is just around the corner, so we must also seek the joy that lies in wait. The happiness. The love. If we don't claim those things, it certainly doesn't keep out the threat of the other."

"No, it doesn't," Roarke said softly.

She touched his cheek, loving how it was rough with stubble, loving how he turned into her palm like he needed to feel her. "I love you," she said. "And there is no wrong moment for that. So if you really want me, if you truly wish to marry me, then I will be yours, Roarke. I will be yours and make you mine every day from this day forward." She lifted up on her tiptoes and kissed him gently. "For the rest of my life."

He caught her around the waist, molding her more firmly to him. He kissed her more deeply, a kiss of relief and joy. A kiss of surrender and peace and a future that was laid out for them at last. With no more secrets or lies or dangers to prevent their happiness.

And she couldn't wait to see what would happen next.

EPILOGUE

Three Months Later

The wedding celebration was in full swing, but it was not Flora and Roarke's. They had not been able to wait and had married in Gretna Green just a week after their engagement had begun. There had been little fanfare and only brief scandal at the surprise union of the former duchess and her husband's nephew. Neither of them had cared about the whispers, having both experienced how tenuous life could be.

And now they stood together watching Valaria and Callum dance, their eyes locked. At last their friends had begun their life together. Flora tucked her arm through Roarke's and looked up at her husband. He looked so much more relaxed and happy now. They, along with his sweet mother and her lovely companion, were tucked into her home in Kent's Row, at least until renovations on their new larger home could be finished.

He had invested a large sum of the money given to him by Thomas into a venture with Grayson Danford that looked to pay enormous dividends. And they only grew to love each other more with every passing day.

She didn't know if she deserved such happiness, she wasn't certain any one person did, but she reveled in it and their future they were planning together, each moment.

"And so you and Valaria are both married," he said, stroking his fingers along hers.

She shivered at the contact and the desire he seemed to inspire with every simple thing. It was wonderful.

"Yes, which means we get to put all our attention onto making sure Bernadette gets her own happy union."

They gazed across the ballroom together and found that Bernadette and Theo were standing together talking. Theo looked almost surprised as he leaned in, listening to whatever she was saying.

"Oh yes," Flora said with a smile. "We have a great deal of work to do there."

Roarke laughed. "I approve of the idea, but I certainly hope you won't put *all* your attention on that endeavor, Mrs. Desmond."

She smiled up at him, just barely resisting the urge to pull him to her and make a spectacle of them both right here in the middle of the ballroom. "I misspoke, my love. I have a great deal of other magical things to keep my attention. And I cannot wait for everything there is to come."

ENJOY AN EXCERPT OF NOT THE DUKE YOU MARRY

BOOK 3 OF THE KENT'S ROW DUCHESSES

The Duchess of Tunbridge had never been a jealous person. It wasn't in Bernadette's nature to covet what others had, nor guard her own possessions or relationships. Certainly, she'd never been one to turn ugly shades of green over the happiness of friends.

And yet she stood at the edge of a ballroom watching one of her dearest friends, Valaria, now the Duchess of Blackvale, dance at her wedding ball with her husband Callum, and Bernadette felt a stir of such an unpleasant emotion. She hated herself for it, because she knew what horrors Valaria had been through and how much she had earned her happy ending with her utterly devoted husband.

She turned away from them and her gaze caught her other best friend instead. Flora Desmond was not dancing with her husband, Roarke, but she, too, looked deliriously happy as they stood close together, their hands linked as they talked together. Flora smiled, blushed a little as Roarke leaned in close to her ear.

Bernadette let out an unsteady sigh and moved away from the happy people celebrating and toward a long table where an alcoholic punch was being served. She took a glass, her third of the night, and swallowed a large mouthful before she got up the courage to turn her attention back to the room and all its happy couples. There was no escaping them, nor the way seeing them made her think and feel.

"That is a sour expression."

She jolted as she was joined in that vulnerable moment by yet another familiar face. Theodore Alexander Monroe Tinsley, the Duke of Lightmorrow, would likely call himself an old friend of hers. In fact, that was often how he introduced himself if they were together at some event. He wasn't incorrect. They had grown up on adjoining estates, after all. Their fathers had been friends and they had often seen each other over the years.

Her marriage to her late husband, the Duke of Tunbridge, had put distance between them. Theo's devotion to being an unattached rake had done the same. And yet they now often found each other thrown together thanks to the courtships and eventual marriages of their mutual friends.

"Good evening, Theo," she said, hoping she didn't sound as sour as he claimed she sounded.

"Etta," he drawled, and she stiffened as tingles moved up her spine both at the seductive tone to his voice and the fact that he used a shortened version of her name. He was the only person left on this earth that called her Etta.

She wasn't sure if she liked that or feared it and the reactions it caused in her.

"You aren't dancing," he said. "May I remedy that?"

She turned toward him to find his hand outstretched and anticipation on his expression. She felt a wild desire to refuse him, to run from the room and the feelings that touching him would inspire. This man made her weak and she knew it, even if she tried to ignore it.

But she couldn't do that, not without making a scene. She didn't need the ramifications of that, certainly Callum and Valaria didn't either. So she swallowed down the rest of her punch, set her cup on a passing servant's tray and put her fingers against his palm. He was warm. She felt that through both their sets of thin gloves. He made no outward reaction to when she touched him, so she schooled her reaction so she would appear just as unmoved.

"Thank you, Your Grace," he said as he guided her to the floor and put his hand against her hip. They began to move together in a waltz and she cursed the universe that it would put her in this position where she had to look up into those dark brown eyes. Ones that seemed to so effortlessly see through everyone around him.

She cleared her throat. "Are you happy for Callum or lamenting his loss of freedom today?"

There was a moment when Bernadette thought she saw some version of regret cross Theo's face, but then it was gone and he smirked a little. God, but he was handsome. He was tall and broad shouldered, with smoldering dark brown eyes and thick brown hair. He was always perfectly groomed and dressed and he always had the attention of every available woman in any room…and some portion of the attached ones, too. Even now ladies watched from every corner, glaring at her for having his interest, even briefly.

"A year or two ago, I admit I might have lamented about his being leg shackled, but I appear to be growing as a person."

She laughed at his playfully frustrated tone. As if growth were a bad thing. "God forbid," she teased. "So you would not say his marriage is a negative now?"

They pivoted and Theo looked off to where Valaria and Callum now stood together. Callum's arm was around her waist and while she spoke to someone, he was just…watching her. And once again, Bernadette felt that pull of jealousy. What would it feel like to have someone look at her that way? To be so entirely focused on her and her happiness and her pleasure? She'd never experienced such a thing, certainly not with her own late husband.

Theo sighed. "He is besotted, and rightfully so. Valaria is not only beautiful, but she is a good match for him. No one could watch what they went through over the last year and not celebrate that they are finally free to be together." He winked at her and the seriousness of his tone melted away. "But if you tell anyone I said that, I will deny it."

"Of course, it will be our secret," she said, and forced a smile.

His brow wrinkled. "So we have established I am reluctantly happy for our friends," he said slowly. "Are you…are you not?" When she drew in a sharp breath, he hastened to add, "I have never seen you be anything but joyful for Valaria and for Flora in their matches. But there is something about your expression. A little glumness at such a happy occasion that doesn't seem *you*."

Oh how she hated how observant this man was. How much he could see through her without even trying even though she meant nothing to him. He played at connection so easily that she couldn't trust it when she saw it shimmering there like a mirage.

"I'm…I'm not glum," she began, trying to meter her tone and knowing she failed when Theo's expression grew sharp.

Now all his focus was on her. "Etta?" he pressed, turning her gently in the crowd of dancers.

She stared up into those eyes and swallowed hard. The music was coming to an end and she needed to make her escape. She stepped from his arms when she could and executed a curtsey. "Thank you for the dance, Theo," she said, and ducked away from him.

She heard him say her name as she left the dancefloor, but she kept going. She went straight through the crowd as far from him as she could manage. Had it not been the dead of winter, she would have fled to the terrace, but all she could do now was hide as best she could.

Only he wouldn't let her. He pushed through the others toward her, his dark gaze locked on her. He paused only to grab two cups of punch from the table and then he came to her. He held out one to her as he arched a brow.

"You can't just run away in the middle of a conversation," he said.

She shook her head. "If you were any kind of gentleman, you would have allowed my escape."

"A gentleman," he teased with a laugh. "Heaven forbid." His tone gentled. "What is it? What is troubling you?"

She sighed. He wouldn't let this go and as much as she knew she could keep it to herself, the words were right there on the tip of her tongue. Ready to wound if they were said to the wrong person. And perhaps it was better to say them to Theo and hope he would protect them.

"I'm happy for them," she whispered, and then drew in an unsteady breath. "But when I look at them it makes me…it makes me..."

"What?"

"Realize how alone I-I am," she stammered, each word heavy on her tongue.

"Ah," he said, and she couldn't help but notice how he angled himself away a fraction. The softness was gone. The connection loosened a little. It reminded her of another conversation they'd once shared, a lifetime ago. He'd turned away from her then, too. "Well, that is to be expected. You've been a widow for a while now, haven't you?"

"Five years," she said softly. "Almost twice as long as I was married in the first place."

"And you're young," he said carefully. "And attractive. Of course you would think about a marriage when all your friends were finding their match. It's natural you'd want that, Bernadette and I'm…I'm sure you'll find someone."

She shook her head. He was saying the right things, she supposed. The same things Valaria and Flora would sometimes say, the same things her parents would say when she was forced to visit them once a month for icy, formal meetings. But when *Theo* said those words, it made her realize something and it bubbled from her lips before she could bid it back.

"It isn't a marriage that I desire," she whispered.

Now his eyes widened. "No?"

"I'm twenty-eight years old and you vastly overestimate my

charms to men looking for a match. And even if one wanted me like that, I don't need their money or their position. I have both of those things on my own. No, it's…it's the…the…" She shook her head. "I suppose I wish that I could take a lover."

Theo had taken his own sip of punch, perhaps to look nonchalant as she stammered and struggled with the words to say something she should have kept to herself, but with that declaration he coughed and sent some portion of the drink bubbling from his lips.

He coughed and wiped the back of his hand across his mouth as he stared at her. "I beg your pardon?"

Out November 14!

ALSO BY JESS MICHAELS

The Kent's Row Duchesses

No Dukes Allowed

Not Another Duke

Not the Duke You Marry (Coming November 14, 2023)

Theirs

Their Marchioness

Their Duchess

Their Countess

Regency Royals

To Protect a Princess

Earl's Choice

Princes are Wild

To Kiss a King

The Queen's Man

The Three Mrs

The Unexpected Wife

The Defiant Wife

The Duke's Wife

The Duke's By-Blows

The Love of a Libertine

The Heart of a Hellion

The Matter of a Marquess

The Redemption of a Rogue

The 1797 Club

The Daring Duke

Her Favorite Duke

The Broken Duke

The Silent Duke

The Duke of Nothing

The Undercover Duke

The Duke of Hearts

The Duke Who Lied

The Duke of Desire

The Last Duke

The Scandal Sheet

The Return of Lady Jane

Stealing the Duke

Lady No Says Yes

My Fair Viscount

Guarding the Countess

The House of Pleasure

Seasons

An Affair in Winter

A Spring Deception

One Summer of Surrender

Adored in Autumn

The Wicked Woodleys

Forbidden

Deceived

Tempted

Ruined

Seduced

Fascinated

To see a complete listing of Jess Michaels' titles, please visit:

http://www.authorjessmichaels.com/books

ABOUT THE AUTHOR

USA Today Bestselling author Jess Michaels likes geeky stuff, Cherry Vanilla Coke Zero, anything coconut, cheese and her dog, Elton. She is lucky enough to be married to her favorite person in the world and lives in Oregon settled between the ocean and the mountains.

When she's not trying out new flavors of Greek yogurt or rewatching Bob's Burgers over and over and over (she's a Tina), she writes historical romances with smoking hot characters and emotional stories. She has written for numerous publishers and is now fully indie and loving every moment of it (well, almost every moment).

Jess loves to hear from fans! So please feel free to contact her at Jess@AuthorJessMichaels.com.

Jess Michaels offers a free book to members of her newsletter, so sign up on her website:

http://www.AuthorJessMichaels.com/

facebook.com/JessMichaelsBks
instagram.com/JessMichaelsBks
bookbub.com/authors/jess-michaels

Made in the USA
Middletown, DE
06 September 2023